Vengeance Upon The Sky

James Leland

ISBN: 979-8-9901309-0-6 (paperback)
ISBN: 979-8-9901309-1-3 (e-book)

Library of Congress Control Number: 2024915886

The story, all names, characters, and incidents portrayed in this production are fictitious. No identification with actual persons (living or deceased), places, buildings, and products is intended or should be inferred.

Publisher's Cataloging-in-Publication data
Names: Leland, James, author.
Title: Vengeance upon the sky / James Leland.
Description: Anaheim, CA: Helios Adventures, 2024.
Identifiers: LCCN: 2024915886 | ISBN: 979-8-9901309-0-6 (paperback) | 979-8-9901309-1-3 (e-book)
Subjects: LCSH Space ships--Fiction. | Interstellar travel--Fiction. | Imaginary wars and battles--Fiction. | Space opera. | Science fiction. | BISAC FICTION / Science Fiction / General | FICTION / Science Fiction / Action & Adventure | FICTION / Science Fiction / Hard Science Fiction | FICTION / Science Fiction / Space Exploration | FICTION / Science Fiction / Space Opera
Classification: LCC PS3612 .E88 V46 2024 | DDC 813.6--dc23

Printed and bound in the United States of America
First printing October 2024

Published by Helios Adventures

If the days were like the nights.
I would be forever blind.
But in the sun I see.
Everything that was meant to be.
- Dr. Janet Avlen

Prologue

One hundred and eighty years ago a revolution in transportation occurred. Humans could finally travel between the stars. Disparate pieces of technology and math came together to allow the gravity engine. Astrophysicists had determined shortly before then that dark matter did not exist. Instead, the stars were not only affected by a long-distance gravity relationship between other stars, but also by a deep gravity well in the curvature of space-time that connected the star to its local gravitational neighbors.

What Albert Einstein and Nathan Rosen did not know, and could not know, but Asbjørn Currier was later able to show is how the heavy celestial bodies such as stars, black holes, and neutron stars were coupled through the space-time metric and not just on it as described by general relativity. Currier's extension led to the Einstein-Rosen-Currier theory, abbreviated ERC.

In ERC, the gravitational well distance of an object was called the Currier depth. It took the equivalent of two stars just under the size of Sol, Earth's sun, to dig holes deep enough through the cosmos to connect create a bridge.

A hypothesis of the new theory was that a high-density mass traveling about ten million miles an hour, relative to the sun, would be able to ride the space-time curvature between the sun and another star. This would come to be known as solar diving.

To travel this way, a new type of starship was needed—one that could harness an ultra-dense mass to deform and stick to the space-time along the boundary of the bridge between stars. Fusion reactors already required exquisite control of electro-magnetic fields. Specialized sensors allowed reading the gravitational paths from the sun to other stars. The only thing missing to create a gravity drive was a small amount of neutronium, the ultra-dense material of a neutron star. Anything less dense would be the size of a planet.

The discovery of a sliver of neutronium in a rarely occurring extra-solar comet led to building the first gravity-drive-enabled sun ship.

Shortly thereafter the rapid expansion of humanity across the galaxy began shaping humanity the way the boom of the industrial revolution, the computer revolution, and the lessons from the failed AI revolution did before.

While sun ships once past the interdiction line could ride the curvature of the gravity well from one star to another, nebulas, free comets, and wandering planets, were all unreachable due to their Currier depth being less than the diameter of the object.

The high-spin neutron stars and quasars were also out of reach due to the lethal amount of electromagnetic energy and radiation. Black holes were visually confusing, the gravity in the local region caused time distortion artifacts with chronometers, and the first mapping expeditions found nothing but dead worlds in orbit.

Researchers that studied solar diving still do not have an answer for diving between the galaxies. The few long-transit maps of the galactic center showed it was a mess. Some amazing pilots, navigators, plotters, and computers were needed just to get around near the galaxy center, let alone get a gravity map of the central well and its counterpoint in another galaxy.

Sky Patrol was created to handle this vast new opportunity. Their charter is to help guide and organize with basic regulatory requirements; provide star mapping; aid research and discovery; and protect as the rescue, police, and military of space.

⚭

Chapter 0. Where Dreams Go To Die

Janet stood up from the half-built, three-meter, metallic-and-epoxy-green sphere that was her research project. It sat three feet above the lab floor and thirty-two feet below the ceiling of the thousand-square-foot Sky Patrol laboratory. The room itself was filled with two fabricators for building custom parts, two primary computer consoles, and a lot of power supply cabling. She looked over at Yasmin, who sat at one of the computer consoles. Her face, partly hidden by long, dark brown hair, glowed from the display. It was sprawling with diagrams of elliptical math, Yasmin's specialty in ERC theory.

Janet walked over to Yasmin and gently put her hand on her shoulder, "How is the shaping equation for the Mini-Sun going?"

"Pretty good. It's like extending magnetic bottle equations. Your original theory gets us most of the way there. Needed to add a few non-linear resonance factors from some of the field-compression effects."

"At some point I'll look over all those adjustments." Janet walked back and leaned on the tool rack next to the drive. "What are you up to this weekend?"

Yasmin turned in her chair. "Saturday me and a few others will be protesting Sky Patrol's proposed intervention on Galtonian."

Janet raised her right brow in question.

Yasmin continued, "It's in the Titus system. It's its own colony rather than a part of the Distributed Worlds System. Apparently, Sky Patrol thinks their government has gone corrupt and has been stealing from local company ventures and damaging the colony's growth."

"I think I heard they want to install some security on planet?"

"Yes, and it's their own planet. The people there can decide. They don't need military police. It will only lead to fighting and violence. And shouldn't be needed," Yasmin replied.

"I do not know enough to comment either way. I am curious. For the few months I have known you, you have been very adamant about peaceful solutions to almost any, if not all, conflicts. How does that work with Sky Patrol having an enforcement wing?"

"I work for the Science Directorate on strictly

fundamental research that isn't likely to lead to any weapons development. I can't help it if Sky Patrol has the biggest collaborative set of research labs and only one of the two working on non-linear gravitational mapping," Yasmin retorted, animating her hands about in annoyance. "The other is on Horizon and doesn't have a focus on travel. Improving life and uncovering God's work amongst the stars is how I can hope we stop having violence, and wars."

"Getting people to cooperatively interact across divided territories faster does seem to have that affect historically. I am hoping for the same with our work here. But I would think protesting to be rather ineffective these days. Would getting a petition before the panel of the Securities Resolution Department not be more effective?" Janet pressed.

"Someone else is doing that. We're out to show our solidarity." Yasmin got up and walked over to Janet and held her hands. "I wish you would come."

"Unfortunately, I cannot. In fact, I was hoping to have you come with me and my friend Vilnus to the Walker Botanical Area. He is on planet for a few days, and I would like you to meet him sometime, but it will have to wait."

"How long have you been friends?"

"About seven years now. We met at a research symposium on Five Star Prime."

"Do you make all your friends at conferences?" Yasmin jested.

"No, goof. Shall we wrap up for today?"

"I'd love to wrap up with you." Yasmin hugged Janet.

Yasmin's hair tickled Janet's mouth, and she could feel Yasmin's bosom pressed into her ribs. Yasmin looked up at Janet with her blue eyes, and Janet leaned down, and Yasmin met her on tiptoes to kiss her.

***

Janet and Vilnus stepped past the visitor entrance to the Walker Botanical Area. The large expanse of silicate pines, imported St. Augustine grass, and patches of Blue Betty flowers were before them, with sandy walkways leading the way.

Vilnus swept his arm across the landscape. "This is the sister garden to the Runner Botanical Area we visited on Five Star Prime. The plants will be different to accommodate the region, but the layout is by the same architect."

Vilnus indicated the path to the left. "Shall we?"

They set off down the path. A patch of Blue Bettys with some orange poppy-looking flowers intermixed decorated the first turn in the path.

"How is your new office on El Ventura working out?" Janet asked.

"It's new to me. Unfortunately, I think they left the furniture from a few decades back. It's really tough stuff, but metallic-gray post-neo-modern is not a fashion style that ever struck me as beautiful. The lack of exterior lighting in the building is a great excuse to take the technology observation assignments. I'm enjoying them rather more than I thought I would."

He leaned over and brushed his hand over the Blue Bettys. "They have an interesting velvety texture."

"I just like how they look and the smell," replied Janet, picking one and holding it to her nose and then out to Vilnus to smell. A small bug landed on Janet's shoulder. He reached over and flicked it off her.

"How are you and Yasmin doing?"

"We are getting along pretty great in the lab. She's brilliant, with a keen grip on elliptic math."

"That's not what I meant. You told me the last part, before you actually met her, while you were listing off interesting conference talks you wanted to see. The part where you get along in the lab is obvious since she's still in your lab. It's the part where you tell me how excited you are about a week's discovery but tellingly leave out what you do afterward. I assume that means you have started seeing someone, and I bet that someone is Yasmin."

Janet blushed. "I . . ."

"Look, it has been a long time since I took you to the violin concert on a date. Many rivers have I crossed since then. I know you don't like to talk about every little dalliance either. I can see you're happy. So I'm happy. If you don't want to tell me all your bottled-up feelings, that's okay."

The silence lingered a little, and they began walking again. They rounded a small hill in the path before Vilnus picked up the conversation again.

"How actually is the research going?"

"We nailed phase two, and we are building phase three now. I'm pretty ecstatic. I wish I could share so much more—"

"About the lab of kiss testing."

Janet slapped his arm, "No. About the research, but Sky Patrol is very particular about this for some reason."

"I get it. I've had the pleasure, or otherwise, of working on some classified projects and really wished I could share. Thinking food?"

"Hungry?" Janet inquired.

"Yes, and there is supposed to be an eatery along this way near a pond that is in the style of food predominate in the area of Five Star Prime where

the sister park is, but they'll have a burger if you're not feeling it."

"Happy either way." Janet smiled back.

"I wish I had a longer stay, to really visit some of the history museums of this planet. Have you been to them?"

"No"—Janet briefly took his hand—"but maybe we will sometime. We have the whole rest of our lives."

***

"It's lit!" Yasmin eeked, and squeezed Janet's hand. They stood in front of the gray sphere that was the foundation of their experiment. The main display showed the thin white-to-orange gradient bar of the main status indicator sitting at idle density. The four hundred other sensors on other displays were also all colored nominal white.

"I will admit I am excited," Janet replied, and squeezed Yasmin around the shoulders.

"Okay, but you have to name it something else. Mini-Sun is not great. Maybe Janet's Ultra-dense Gravity Source."

Janet looked at her. "I am not calling it that."

"Too bad, I liked Janet's JUGS." Yasmin frowned. "How about Sunspot, like the dog name and the star surface feature?"

"Cute. Seems a better commercial name, albeit probably for conveyance, not an engine enhancement. We need a good science name. Maybe JY-1?"

"Q-JAYS! For Quarent – Janet and Yasmin's Sphere."

"I think that is great. Has a bird-like feel, and it is for flying beyond the stars. Now, let us see if we can get the energy density inside this Q-JAY up to the metric sense point."

She reached out to the console and started the test sequence. Incrementally, the energy density of the sphere began climbing. The green bar crept to the right on the display, slowly approaching the second marker labeled Threshold Density, just shy of the third and last mark on the line labeled Metric Contact.

"It's still stable," Yasmin commented. "Glad to see we're not testing the thermal safety dump today. I'll keep watching the status if you want to begin the petition to move us to the Leonard Institute orbital lab."

She glanced up at Janet, who was smiling.

"I wrote it two days ago," Janet answered.

***

The small probe Janet was holding clanged on the composite floor of the orbital lab. The tinkling sound touching across the metal equipment, structures, and screens and into the ears of Yasmin.

"Dang it, Janet, you startled me! Are you okay?"

"I tore the gravity lace."

Janet slumped sideways in her chair. She looked back down at the ruined golden-silicate mesh that was integral to forming gravity maps. She looked over at Yasmin, who was just standing from her console.

"No sorrow dance, please," Janet asked. "I am actually upset this time. Very tired of getting defective test parts."

"Defective? Could you have damaged it? You know normally only robots put these down into the casing, not to be touched again?"

"No, it was a crystalline fracture. The lace is supposed to be amorphous, but it had a crack, not a tear, appear when it broke. We need a good lace, and this rejected junk isn't helping."

Janet stood up. "I am going to go take the lab's working gravity drive."

"You will probably break that too," Yasmin warned.

"I appreciate the confidence, but I have done this a few times before." She looked up in recollection. "I was inspecting the metric sensor of the gravity drive in my graduate lab. I had separated out a number of parts. Dr. Ahar, my professor, was both very irritated and then surprised when I got it back together in working condition."

She paused in her story. "Want to come steal it with me?"

"You bet," said Yasmin, stretching out her limbs.

*

Back in the lab with their pilfered gravity drive set up in an open corner. Janet ran the continuity sensor over her work.

"I have the lower-level interface to the gravity lace in the star drive installed. If you could check it when you have a pause," Janet said.

Yasmin popped up from her chair and walked over to where Janet sat. The cover, undercover, control electronics, and power manifold had been removed, and the silver-looking box that extended the gravity lace backward from the normal direction it would face, toward the neutronium core of a sun ship. Yasmin picked up the micro-inspector and walked it past the interface. She reached out, and Janet handed her the continuity sensor.

"I don't see any issues on the sensors." Yasmin walked back to her display and tapped one of the buttons. "Nor does the scan algorithm." She faced Janet. "Sorry I said you were doing it wrong

earlier. You're always so good with your hands."
She winked.

Janet squeezed her shoulder. "Let us put this
together and run the diagnostics."

A few hours later the complete gravity drive was
chained together at its back end with the sphere of
the Q-JAY.

"Let us boot it up," Janet said, and Yasmin tapped
on the display.

"The sun ship navigation program is talking
with the gravity drive. No errors reported." Yasmin
pushed the display up on the main display in
the lab. She pushed another button, and the test
sequence started.

Janet watched the green line showing the energy
density of the Q-JAY creeping up. Six minutes later
it reached the Pre-Dive line. The program let the
energy sit for a minute, verifying the system stability, and then moved up one notch to Matrix
Sense. The wall monitor running the navigation
program bloomed from the stored map to being
alive with new flowing information of a constantly
updating gravity map.

The map showed the gravity well of Mota, the
sun star system, and the other two star wells that
tunneled to it. The wonderous living plot showed
the grids of the connecting transits beyond the

adjoining gravity wells, and the elliptic markings with their interdiction points highlighted the navigation program thinking they were much closer to the sun than they were.

They caught their breath watching the gravity map.

"Oh heavens. We can map the gravity metric from anywhere. We did it!" Yasmin jumped into the air and grabbed Janet around the waist.

Janet felt the shared energy of pride in that moment.

"Damn right, we did," Janet replied, pulling Yasmin in with her arm and leaning down and kissed her fully.

The chime on the lab door interrupted Janet's moment of euphoria. She went to answer it. The room displays went blank, hiding the research from anyone other than Janet and Yasmin. She opened the door to Captain Deneau, the director of the Leonard Institute.

He leaned over, slightly looking around Janet, "I wondered who took the institute's test engine."

"We were getting junk parts, and no sense in delaying if it was not in use at the moment. Is that why you are here?"

"No. I got good news for you two. Sky Patrol is going to schedule a drone and a class III nav-

igation research sun ship if you send the Science Directorate a report of a working demonstration."

Janet looked over at Yasmin, who had walked up next to the door also. "We got a ship?"

"You will nine months after the initial demonstration, yes. Time to do an integration on the drone, its test, and then installation on the sun ship if successful. Since you're past rejected parts, how much longer do you need the institute's engine?"

"Two days, I think," Janet replied.

"Two? That close to a demo report?"

"Oh, we got it. Now we just need to write it up."

The director's eyes widened a little. "Please put the engine back in three days in case you—" he cleared his throat "—need more time. I'll send the report request to your pad directly so you can feed it to the lab's computer."

Janet stretched out her left arm with the pad on it, and the director tapped the work pad he was carrying to hers. Captain Deneau left, and they stood in silence for a moment after the door closed.

"We have a ship," Janet uttered.

Yasmin skipped around the lab. "We have a ship!"

Chapter 1. Is There In Truth No Beauty?

Strapped into her shuttle seat, Janet gazed out at the sun ship *Galileo*. The surface of its white spherical hull floated out amongst the stars. Little hints of sparkling light glittered off its surface. The small dots of sensors started appearing into view as they approached. She could see two radar panels wrapped over both the forward and backward surfaces. A series of closed window ports were arranged in various places.

Like all sun ships, it was a sphere wrapped around a neutron core. This one belonged to Sky Patrol and was a class III navigation research ship, 210 meters in diameter.

Her comforting bed held her for less time than usual this morning. Janet had watched the awaking light of sunrise on Merideth-Standly Main, the primary planet in the Merideth-Standly solar system. The trip over from planet was typical, but this was the first time a sun ship and all its capabilities had been reserved for her.

The Sky Patrol uniform she wore was the purple jumpsuit of the Science Directorate, complete with matching belt, pockets, and utility lamp on her left side just below collar height. Touching her upper sleeve, she felt four gold bars. Two horizontal solid bars on the bottom indicated the rank of senior scientist—the equivalent of lieutenant in the command ranks. On the top, spaced equidistant to the lower bars, was a dashed double bar that indicated a temporary promotion to senior scientist-commanding. Which, for the purpose of ensuring mission safety, put her at a rank just below captain of the vessel.

It will be a good day, Janet thought.

Janet stepped off the shuttle at half gravity and into a hug from Yasmin. She hugged her back and looked down at Yasmin, who wore a matching purple uniform without the commander's double bar.

"Nice surprise," Janet said.

Yasmin gently stepped back, still holding her hands.

"I'm excited. We're finally here. Or almost here. I know we've got two more weeks before we really do the test," Yasmin answered.

"Are we ready for this?'" Janet asked, the lighter gravity of the outer deck starting to give her butterflies in her stomach.

"I think you are. I'm the one who's always worrying. Here . . ." Yasmin squeezed Janet's hands briefly and closed her eyes. "If I take the wings of the dawn. If I dwell in the depths of the stars. Even there Your hand will lead me. If I say, 'Surely the darkness will overwhelm me, and the light around me will be dim,' for the darkness is not dark to You, and the light always bright. For darkness and light are alike to You. God shepherd us."

Yasmin squeezed Janet's hands again and opened her eyes.

"Ready to spend two weeks with me?" Yasmin asked.

Smiling down, Janet said, "Yes, I am," and kissed her.

"It will be nice not being in a rush of work. Just monitoring Q-JAY, maintenance, and cuddling. You know, I'm surprised you didn't miss your own experiment for sleep," joked Yasmin, letting go of her embrace.

"Do not blame me if you get up two hours before any normal shift," Janet retorted.

They slide down the ladder to the working deck with standard gravity. She turned Yasmin around toward the direction of the bridge and tapped her on the butt.

"Let us go brief the crew. I will be bright and excited when the time comes. And I will take the prerogative as lead scientist of declaring my own shift all I want."

"You were bright and excited so much last month, it seemed like you wanted to go ride the drone ships yourself," Yasmin answered.

"Yes, and compared to this last year, the next two weeks are going to feel like we are traveling as slow as a blimp," Janet agreed.

"What's a blimp?" Yasmin replied.

"Vilnus is a history fan. We went hot-air ballooning on a trip to Larado. You sit in a carriage under a large envelope filled with hot air and let the wind blow you to a new place. The way you experience the view is incredible. He shared that a blimp is basically a very large balloon used for transport. In this case, the air displacement is usually done with helium, and you can carry things with it. It's a painfully slow method of transport."

"Sounds boring. I much prefer to be able to look out viewports. The planets. And to check out Uranus," Yasmin replied.

"Leave my butt out of this, even if you do like it," Janet said.

"I swear that's a motto on a space dock somewhere," Yasmin laughed.

"What will you be filling your idle research time with?" Janet asked.

"I brought several volumes of Charlotte Brontë to read. I've been working my way backward through historical point-of-view literature. I just finished *On Walden Pond*. It was about a man who didn't like city life, so he pretended to live like a remote explorer," Yasmin replied.

"When were those written?"

"Pre-nineteen hundred."

Janet groaned. "I have trouble with anything written more than a hundred years ago. How do you not know what a blimp is?"

"Admittedly, I skipped a hundred years from before two thousand. A lot was dark war stuff, and I wanted reflection and discovery."

"Want to know something funny? Vilnus was telling me that twentieth-century sci-fi writers loved the concept of faster-than-light speed and were always making up methods that defied physics. You know, if this experiment works as it did on the drone ships, a bunch of your research may not be needed."

"True, but I'm still pleased I did it. It got you to come to my talk fourteen months ago, after all. Who knew 'Hyperbolic Celestial Navigation Using Oblique Star-Dive Entry Points' would be such a lure for attractive women."

"It sounded fascinating, and the talk was intriguing. And your extension has allowed the drive-control program to work for this test." Janet paused and turned to look at Yasmin in the corridor. "I am truly pleased you took me up on my offer to join me."

"Agreed! I like that our research prospects are growing with us. Glad we can do this together. Most people don't share chief interests."

They arrived at the bridge. The bridge was oversized for a class III science vessel. Tailored for navigation research, it was designed with normal command, navigation, and operations, and also the primary research on the bridge. Continued experience showed that computer algorithms were best for calculation and post-analysis, but poor at clever responses to new situations or collaborative approaches that the crew brought.

The large circular room was surrounded by a continuous set of screens. The pilot's station was located in front of the primary view screen. The navigation officer was stationed to the forward right with star and system charts on his display. Ship operations on the forward left showed the gravity drive status, fusion reactor, and structural stresses. Auxiliary research was set up along the back wall of screens. The captain's console was in the middle, with the station set up to rotate around the room. Pilot, navigation, and research could coordinate without the barrier's imposed screen or the risk of network failure.

Captain Helena was seated in her command blue uniform with the gold captain's star and two double command bars emblazoned on her sleeve. She stood and made introductions. The pilot, Mr. Davis, sat serenely at his console. Oren was at Navigation. He turned and nodded at Yasmin and smiled at Janet. Abigail was focused on her operation board. Dr. Hall stood behind Abigail. All four wore the standard gray of Sky Patrol sun ship operations officers.

Captain Helena motioned to Janet. "You may begin the mission brief when you are ready." Yasmin went and sat at a research station.

"Thank you, Captain," Janet walked to the left of the main view. She typed in her access code on the pad wrapped on her left arm and tapped her arm to the operations consol.

"I appreciate you being here to support this research project. Let me introduce myself. I am Dr. Janet Avlen. My current line of research, and this experiment, is in extending gravity-drive capability and solar-dive transport. And I hope it will be the next step in inter-solar system transit. In particular, this may be an enabler for transiting to locations without deep gravity wells."

Mr. Davis raised an eyebrow, but everyone listened patiently.

Janet brought up a concept map on the main view screen. She continued, "The two star systems for this test will be Merideth-Standly in the lower left and Empty-47 on the upper left, with the primary test at Empty-47. We will depart Merideth-Standly after Yasmin, in the back, and I augment the gravity drive with a device we are calling Q-JAY.

"The lone star Empty-47 has been selected for this experiment because as the convenience label indicates, it has no large masses in orbit and very few captured objects. Essentially, there are no secondary gravity curvatures. Verification of the installed performance and coupling with *Galileo*'s gravity drive and the emergency power-down system will take place on arrival at Empty-47.

"After initial checkout, we will use the gravity drive to place two weeks of ship time, or a half a billion miles between *Galileo* and Empty-47. That will put us here at this dotted circle upper right on the diagram." An arrow appeared between Empty-47 and the circle. "The two-week distance is to unambiguously prove the point that the gravity well of the star was not the mechanism of transport."

Oren interrupted. "Of transport? It takes a star just under the size of Sol to warp space-time deep enough through the cosmos to allow diving between stars using an Einstein-Rosen tunnel through space. That's with a sufficiently large mass of neutronium to distort the tunnel to allow the ship through and the gravity drive to ride the curvature of the gravity well. You're suggesting you can drive the energy density high enough to provide that bridge?"

Janet looked at Oren. "Yes. The Q-JAY's purpose is to provide a mobile gravity well deep enough to bridge the gap from any location to any other location that can be mapped. This will allow us to leap between the two systems, just like any other normal gravity drive does between two stars. To spoil the reveal, the purpose of this particular test is to take a sun ship from a nearly flat gravity metric and return to a star." She brought an arrow down from the dotted circle to the Merideth-Standly system. "Use of the Q-JAY gravity well will be called free diving to distinguish it from normal solar diving."

The captain spoke up. "Have there been other tests for safety?"

Janet nodded. "There have been two miniature drone tests out of the Empty-47 solar region, both with the same Q-JAY device that will be used for this test taken by the drone currently in the holding bay. They proved this would work on a small scale, and it is safe for a fully equipped research ship to make the attempt. To answer the earlier question, it is possible to create an energy density sufficient to make an Einstein-Rosen tunnel for solar diving. During installation checkout and at the trial run, we will be able to observe the gravity map form and update as with any typical solar dive."

"Noted. Any effects to the drone ship?" Helena replied.

"All nominal results. The only difference will be our free dive distance from Empty-47," Janet confirmed.

Oren nodded. "I look forward to trying it. Maybe I can go check out some nebulas and rogue comets with it. Or jump galaxies and avoid that gravitational mess that makes up the galactic center. I mean, you can't even read those transit maps."

Janet smiled. "I hope so too. Now, the star pair was chosen because in an emergency, a flare drone that we will leave parked around Empty47 will solar dive, allowing Sky Patrol to send help and return us to the fleet-repair facility we are at.

"On our scheduled return, there will be a Sky Patrol rescue-and-recovery vessel awaiting halfway between our arrival spot in the Merideth-Standly star system and Main. Their instructions will be to contact , but their sensors will at our arrival location to obscure our arrival method.

"Let me remind you as I have been reminded: this is a classified experiment. And the fundamental technology of the inner workings of the device is at a different classification than the general experiment. Access to the Q-JAY is restricted to Yasmin and myself. Until authorized by Sky Patrol to discuss the details, we are just a Sky Patrol navigation research vessel off on normal navigation research. Any questions?"

The crew acknowledged the briefing.

Helena waited a polite amount of time. "Looks like everyone is ready to begin. Janet, is the install of Q-JAY here or at Empty?"

"The timeline is available on the mission calendar and can be adjusted as needed. For the install, we do the installation here. I will have to briefly take the gravity drive offline, and Q-JAY is otherwise inert in the off state. The install should be about five hours, and we can start the journey part of the mission tomorrow."

Helena replied, "Please begin the install with Yasmin. Abigail, please monitor ship status during the process. And the rest of the crew is dismissed until tomorrow."

***

Janet took her seat at the main science station next to Yasmin. "No issues in installation, Captain."

Captain Helena touched her consol. "Mission phase two logged as starting. Abigail, please signal to Transit Control that we're departing as scheduled. Mr. Davis, take us to Empty-47."

A few minutes later they departed from parking orbit. There was a subtle shift in weight as the sun ship's drive began pulling them toward the Merideth-Standly sun. In just a few hours they would solar dive using the gravity well that reached between the two neighbor stars.

Janet watched the view of the solar dive passively.

"You look bored," Yasmin inquired.

"I prefer to see planets from space, or observe them from the orbital launch rockets, where you can see the vast expanses of a planet's structure at once."

"I wondered why you never seemed to pay attention to the solar dives we have been on before. It's my first time on a sun ship bridge though. The view with all the extra details is very interesting."

"Slightly more than normal, I will give you that," Janet answered.

Traveling at two percent of light, using the gravity drive to pull them ever rapidly toward the star, they were nearing the interdiction line where they could solar dive. As they approached the outer corona, the sensors started losing cohesion from the extreme electrical and magnetic fluxes.

This was very familiar, like every solar dive she had done before, with the same readings at her station as those dives where she had access to navigation data. Entries and exits from the dive points were marked on the map with scheduled transits in populated systems. The navigation map shifted from static to a living gravity map. It began forming on both navigation and the main screen, allowing them to see the actual gravity wells and confirm all the destination stars available from their dive point.

Oren spoke up. "No issues. Map is live."

Mr. Davis replied, "Confirmed, no issues. Commit or escape?"

Captain Helena responded, "Commit."

Mr. Davis pushed the dive commit handle forward. The solar dive started, and the outside world visibly disappeared, leaving a teal color glowing lightly from the screen as the high energy densities were pushed away. There was no light in the drive stream except that emitted from the gravity-drive shaping field acting as a form of shield working to keep the ship safe. The inertial freeze from the isotropic gravity of the Einstein-Rosen tunnel held them in place as if they were surrounded by thick foam. Then, after about twenty seconds, they tore through the other side, streaming up from the star of Empty-47, sixteen light years away from Merideth-Standly.

A few minutes later, Abigail spoke up. "Captain, the flare drone has been deployed at the station. We've reached the forty million miles mark, and all readings nominal."

"Q-JAY check out coordinates location in about fifteen minutes," Oren added.

The ship stopped accelerating and began coasting on inertial momentum.

Janet asked, "Permission to proceed with the Q-JAY integration test and safety check of the emergency power dump?"

"Granted," replied the captain, tapping her consol.

The permission locks on Janet's screen turned green. She verified the release interlock on the gravity drive. She started the power density ramp on the Q-JAY. The density climbed up toward metric sense.

"Would you look at that," Oren announced.

They all turned to look at the navigation screen. It had come alive with the real-time gravity map.

"Impressive," the captain responded.

"The test protocol has us hold that for five minutes, and then we begin the safety check."

They waited, staring, as they could see the traffic

pattern in and out of Merideth-Standly well outside the interdiction line.

"Permission to proceed with safety tests?"

"Granted," the captain said.

"Starting the emergency power dump," Janet announced, and touched her console.

The main screen shifted to a video feed of their ship from the flare drone, and operations shifted to showing the relative power density of Q-JAY and the temperature of the power dissipation rings. Then a massive inrush of current was pushed back through the gravity drive's emergency power-release safety system.

Abigail's jaw dropped. "The plan detailed the current level, but is that even safe?"

"The jacket is rated for thrice the expected need, more than the briefing said the limit was. You can see the temperature of the thermal belt is leveling," Janet answered. "However, I would say it is distinctly not safe for anything near us."

The drone video showed the power dissipation rings that the ship was jacketed in, including the auxiliary ring installed for this mission, were glowing white-hot approaching X-ray emissions.

"The kind of thing you usually never want to see," the captain mentioned. "I remember the safety talk in command training briefing for its history. That original sun ships only had thermal belts sufficient for waste heat. That is, until the gravity drive of one ship lost two of its power lines at once and the backlash current melted all but the ship's framing."

"But certainly beautiful in this case. A seventy-minute light show," Janet said. "Readings are at expected values. Looks like there will be no stability problems for the trip. And if everything is back to nominal at that time, then we are ready for our journey."

***

Janet walked into the engineering bay. Yasmin was already there admiring the systems. The Q-JAY sitting in front of Yasmin locked under its tamper container painted with two dancing jesters as the temporary logo. Only the power and control conduits emerged from the container. They were wired to a four-meter-diameter half cylinder on the floor containing the upper half of the intricate gravity-shaping mechanism that was the gravity drive. The status screen on the gravity drive simply showed the gravity field of the neutronium core and the secondary effect of Empty-47 slowly dying away.

Yasmin looked up at Janet. "Thing of beauty. Are we really going to have two jesters as the logo?"

"It was your idea, and it is half accurate," Janet replied.

"It's not. I am a super-serious researcher, and you don't have a hat like that at all. I think we should paint a scantily clad lady on it like they did in one of the war books I was reading before I quit twentieth-century books."

"Why not? But it might not go over well with sales."

"Too bad. I was thinking they could paint me."

Janet smiled at Yasmin. "You would."

Yasmin continued, "When we run the experiment, do you think we will see any of the odd space luminance readings the drones did?"

"I do not know. We did not when we ran the metric sense test. I am not super worried about it. Light does funny things when you start bending space-time. We will find out when the flare drone left in orbit around Empty47 transits back. I hope we look like a massive starburst."

"Or like we have the wings of a Valkyrie?" Yasmin mused.

"That would be something. I'm glad I attended your colloquium," Janet responded.

Yasmin walked over and kissed her. "It's times I like this that I feel blessed by the Creator."

***

At chart counting time 2050804, two weeks after arrival in the Empty-47 star system, Captain Helena came out to the bridge and sat in the command chair. She looked individually at Janet, Yasmin, Mr. Davis, Oren, and Abigail. Dr. Hall arrived on the lift and joined them.

Yasmin asked, "How are the Halls of Medicine today?"

"Oh, funny," the doctor replied.

The captain began the briefing. "Today is finally that day. We made it beyond our flat-metric criteria about twenty minutes before the predictions."

Yasmin interjected, "It just means Empty-47 has been shedding stellar plasma faster than the model of the system predicted. So we had a little wind at our backs. As you can imagine, this isn't a popular system to study and update the database on."

The captain continued, "We have not received any negative update on the arrival point at Merideth-Standly. We are past the time limit when we can receive such a message, so we are go for dive at fourteen hundred."

It was time to prove years of research right. *Here is my career, my life. Let us jump*, thought Janet.

The meeting went quickly, and they began doing a rundown on the full system status, reconfirming that all the parts were operating. The expedition had brought a spare of everything, as they all knew just how easy it was for the ever-present Murphy and his law to be a jerk and wreck a perfectly good mission. And between now and docking at MeridethStandly Main, Janet and everyone else, she suspected, prayed they didn't have to open a single repair kit.

Thirty minutes later, at thirteen fifty-seven, *Galileo*'s pilot, Mr. Davis, announced the time. *Time is here,* thought Janet, and felt her breath.

Janet and Yasmin locked eyes and then turned to their auxiliary research station displays. Janet's display showed all the readings of Q-JAY, the ship's fusion drives, and the gravity drive. Yasmin's was decorated with the gravity map in multiple formats.

"Status for diving to Merideth-Standly," requested Captain Helena.

"Confirmed. Primary dive computer is interfaced to the Q-JAY," replied Abigail.

"Confirmed, gravity map successfully formed. We are live. Plotting to Merideth-Standly," Oren answered from navigation.

"Confirmed, Q-JAY readings level. Safe to free dive," announced Janet.

Janet and Yasmin turned and looked at the main display with the gravity map and stellar maps spread across the entire front display. Yasmin commented to Janet, "It is so unreal, seeing this on a sun ship far from nowhere. But to see, to feel it in person."

"Fourteen hundred ship time. Sixteen thirty-seven Merideth-Standly local time. Commit or escape?" requested Mr. Davis.

"Commit to dive," Helena ordered.

The pilot pushed the dive commit handle forward, and all of a sudden gravity didn't feel right; it almost hurt.

No light, no, no, no, no, no, Janet's mind went off. Then her time perception disappeared.

Chapter 2. Light Amongst The Stars

Vilnus stood on the balcony of the Linus Research Facility, facing the mountain range a few kilometers away. It was the kind of view someone would paint: the slanted sandstone cliffs strutting from the sagebrush and dirt. Snow was still melting off the tips of the hills. A herd of grandos, four-legged beasts with three curled horns, grazed the grass meadow below the facility. The breeze was just right for daydreaming. Vilnus had visited a similar countryside on Larado with Janet. It was a beautiful world with unusual mountain formations and was covered in forests and green plains. He smiled, recalling with fondness the trip and his traveling companion, Janet.

They had hit it off immediately at a meeting on Five Star Prime, seven years ago. He was there from Sky Patrol answering questions on how to use a newly developed coating to reduce thermal loading near the communications arrays on solar observation platforms. At the time, Janet was experimenting with a specialty metal for energy storage. He asked her on a date, but that went nowhere for reasons outside his control. But they were fast friends. Janet couldn't go into the details of her research. But Vilnus understood, in principle, that it was to solve the problem of solar diving without a deep gravity well.

He smiled, thinking about their trip to Larado and Janet's incredulous disbelief in his desire to try tent camping and not use lodging or sleeping booths.

"You get closer to the ground, you get to enjoy some air, you see stars," Vilnus had waxed on about the beauty of more primitive ways to stay out in nature.

Janet had argued, "I can see and feel all of that before I get in the sleeping booth, but there will be no deer poop below me."

"No deer poop. It's just dirt," Vilnus had retorted.

"Deer pooped there."

"Maybe, not recently."

"Still, deer poop." Janet crossed her arms, smiling.

"Then in that sleep of smell what dreams may come," offered Vilnus.

"Death, not smell, it is death," Janet had replied.

Vilnus smiled, looked up from the beasts, and left the balcony, back into the conference complex. He caught a group of researchers from different companies and Sky Patrol gathering for the tour headed to the lab area of the facility. After the labs, he was rather looking forward to the tour of the fabrication facility that was the home of the Linux Motors and Rockets complex.

The guide asked them all to stick close before introducing the first lab. "As you will recall from history class, which I'm sure you all took, it was the lucky capture of a comet surrounding neutronium that allowed the building of the first gravity drive. That then allowed our sun ships to have both gravity and the ability to solar dive to another system. Here, we hope to make a similar improvement in getting ships off planet. Yes, atomic motors are incredibly efficient, but what if we could set up a shaped gravity pipe using a modification of the gravity drive and a stationary neutronium gravity source? It would very much speed up the trip between surface and orbit, particularly for small deliveries."

Bullshit idea, Vilnus thought. He really wanted to see the researchers show more than just a simulation. An actual experiment would be better. That is, if they could get their toy model to behave itself. The guide explained that the actual experiment was on the Linus orbital station safely in space to avoid the pellet sinking through the planet. The planet would be fine, but you would lose your pellet. So far, the neutronium pellet kept pulling all manner of test objects right into the pellet itself, leaving a slightly bigger pellet.

Vilnus imagined having your transport ship being compacted to constituent neutrons at the end of the trip seemed like a poor form of transport.

He also knew neutronium was potentially very hazardous; it was the densest material in the universe. Sun ships were as much about protecting the outside environment from the neutronium as they were about travel. If enough was brought together, you risked building a mass of sufficient size that it would act like its own planet, disrupting orbits and possibly merging with anything nearby. However, the modern neutronium-mining ships with their laser chippers would probably be able to prevent that.

The group left the labs and walked across a sky bridge five stories in the air to the lower floors of the assembly building. They proceeded to a lift to the fifteenth floor. Standing on the balcony overlooking the two-kilometer-long fabrication facility was awe-inspiring. On the far left of where he stood, he could see the interior atomic energy core of the rockets being assembled. Inside the scaffolding was the fusion reactor being prepped for installation.

The guide described the pearlescent-blue material that coated the reactors was a "very thin layer of ruthenium complex to help align the magnetic fields, so the fields remain parallel to the surface in order to prevent long-term deterioration and deviations of the atomic magnetic bottle."

They walked for a few minutes, and halfway down the assembly line, he could see the exterior pipes being attached to the reactor. *For such a beautiful assembly line, this is one boring interior. No pictures, no people, no color other than gray,* thought Vilnus. At the far end of the assembly line, it looked like housing was being wrapped over the whole device.

The guide interjected, "At the end of the assembly line, housing is being wrapped around the entire atomic motor. It serves two purposes: that of preventing other objects from damaging critical components, and as the last barrier should the magnetic bottle break. The shield can handle the melted slag that would remain in all the interior components. In the last two hundred years of atomic rocket flight, the bottle has only broken twice, so don't leave safety at home."

Vilnus spoke up, "I saw a daslet sign over there. May I be excused for a minute?"

The guide frowned and appeared to glance at the

Sky Patrol emblem embroidered on his shirt. "Go ahead. We won't be far down the walk."

Vilnus turned down the offshoot and into the parallel corridor. *No extra security, apparently. Too little, I should have had another escort.* He saw a computer terminal halfway to the daslet. He leaned against it to look at his pad. *You're not hiding things, are you, Linus?* He glanced back in the hallway in the reflection of his pad and, with his right hand, pulled out a little gray disk about two fingers wide and dropped it on the console. The Patrol Medallion could retrieve any data on a system so long as the computer had some kind of Sky Patrol authority system on it. Less well known was that the medallion could also access a great many systems that did not have authority systems. The medallion had a little green circle on the top that spun around and turned red, indicating it was done. He pocketed it. *Too bad you can't tell me what you've spied on for Sky Patrol.* The data would be offloaded and sent to Sky Patrol Security when he was back in orbit and not tied up with the tour.

He ducked into the daslet quickly, washed his hands, and walked back to the tour. They would finish in a few minutes, and dinner with some of the more interesting researchers was his schedule.

***

"They will never know there was a taco."

"You kill me, Gregor. This is why I like coming to these research events. Now, since that's true, hand them over," replied Vilnus ecstatically. "I'm famished."

"So, when are you leaving?" the lead researcher asked, bringing his attention back to the conversation.

"I have a spaceport launch on Friday. Tomorrow I will spend some time exploring the mountains. Not every facility is so beautifully placed," answered Vilnus between tacos.

"Remind me, which part of Sky Patrol are you in?" asked one of the other researchers.

"Sensor Research," replied Vilnus, "everything from the low frequency, such as radar used for mapping the debris in orbit, all the way to communication lasers."

"And what did you think of our talk on hypergravity communication?" asked Gregor.

"It would be fascinating if you could get it to work. It would be nice to not have to send messenger drones through the solar wells. It's as if we still use the Pony Express."

Gregor and a few others looked puzzled.

"The Pony Express was a mail service on Earth several hundred years ago. You would have someone ride a horse, a fast four-legged beast about two meters tall, if you haven't seen one, with a satchel of messages from town to town. They hadn't invented electronic communications yet."

"Ah, so the breakdown in the electronic transmission is like switching over to physical delivery halfway through," Gregor reiterated.

"Yes. And it would be especially nice if you could get any hyper-gravity device to fit on a sun ship and not just on a planet station," Vilnus answered.

"Since sun ships can only transit between star systems at the star's gravity well, the ships will always be near star systems. Does it make sense that you would need this communication on ships?" asked Gregor.

The question made him think of Janet's research endeavors she summarized as not binding solar dives to stars. "I could see uses on ships. Just cutting down light lag for ships on extended-distance runs on the edge of the system," Vilnus replied.

"More wine?" the waiter interrupted.

***

A day later, Vilnus strapped himself into one of the two hundred passenger chairs of the orbital rocket. The atomic motors pushed the craft skyward. A pressure of three times the force of gravity weighed on him for several minutes during launch. Then the pressure was back to standard gravity when riding up to midlevel orbit, where the sun ships orbited. The sun ships could travel the interconnected gravity wells between solar systems, but landing them with their neutron cores was a bad idea. The core may have had the ship's framing for protection, but neutronium was always a risk, and you compounded that by putting the containment under stress.

Something of a pleasant ride, Vilnus thought—a touch of exhilaration, even if it was routine travel at this point. The trip to the Linus research venue had been interesting. As usual, the weather had been good, and it was nice to get away from normal work every few months.

Vilnus boarded the sun ship and went to his cabin. While he was resting in his cabin, the ship began its transit to the solar dive point. He was reading an article Jim, a friend of his who was into ship design, had sent. The article was on a new research-class ship for exploring newly discovered star systems of interest. The new ship was a massive piece of work. It was a big, beautiful sphere, sixteen hundred meters in diameter. Like all solar-diving-capable ships, the interior had an empty area one hundred meters in diameter inside the center where the gravitational attraction of the neutronium core was too high. The distance also allowed the gravitational forces to be balanced by the gravity drive's reaction forces. The gravity drive, besides propulsion, was used to keep the core in place so the ship didn't just sink into itself or other things, like the researchers at Linus kept doing with their test objects. Then deck after deck circled the core, past the eight working decks where gravity was within ten percent of standard, until the exterior decks were reached. Those decks were mostly filled with sensors of every type. What was unusual was the ship held a collection of eight smaller exploratory ships that could be manned and would work their way through the star system being explored. Typically, manned auxiliary ships were a feature on Sky Patrol capital ships and freight ships, as drone ships were .

Vilnus looked up at the time. He was pleased to see that it was only a few minutes before the ship began the multi-star system dive between this star system and his destination. Unfortunately, he didn't have bridge clearance on standard passenger transports like he did on the Sky Patrol ships. The screen on the recreation deck was the only place where the view would be impressive. The cabin projection was less exciting, and the regular viewports had closed an hour ago to avoid blinding everyone with the sun's light and overwhelming the thermal cyclers. *Oh well*, he thought. He had seen suns before.

He tossed the article reader aside and picked up a paper book with a bright-colored illustration. The cover featured a lady and gentleman in purple space suits, set against a backdrop of a glass-domed Martian surface hued in red, yellow, and blue. The man was pointing at a rocket shaped like a pointed ellipse with wings, and the lady was holding a blaster. The story was written long before he was alive, but the imagination of the writer was spot on for the atomic rockets that took people to orbit, but not so accurate about the universe being populated with aliens. A harrowing tale of exploration. *Adventures are written about people who probably didn't want them*, thought Vilnus.

The dive indicator lights flashed on around the room's periphery, and seconds later, he felt the inertial freeze that came with being in transit in a solar dive.His body was still, as was everything else. He could still see.

No sound, however, as all the objects in the ship were fixed in place by the interplay of the gravity drive and the shaped gravity inside the well. Seconds later, the solar dive and the related sensations ended. Each actual dive would only last a few seconds. The longest commercial dive he knew about was just over one minute.

After a few dives and four hours of realigning the ship around the various stars for the consecutive solar dives, they cleared the last solar dive to the El Ventura system, the location of his current home planet. A message loaded in from Janet when the ship made a communication link with the system.

She had been crying. He had never seen her like that.

> *Hi, Vilnus. Sorry I have been out of touch lately. How is your trip so far? Anyway, would you like to come to Horizon Four with me? I have a serious problem. I cannot talk about it, but I would appreciate the company. I am feeling lonely out here.*

Chapter 3. It Depends On Who You Know

Oswald walked into the main auditorium of the Interstellar Cartography and Transport Symposium. Looking around the room, he noticed two large banners hanging in the corners of the room. They had a golden compass centered in a blue stripe between two red bars on the edges, further trimmed with a gold edge. Minus the gold border, it was the same design the patch on his green uniform had. He was here as part of Sky Patrol Cartography to catch up various commercial ventures and research labs on what was on the horizon for better transportation.

Walking past a few of multiple aisles of gray chairs, he took a seat most of the way back. Oswald looked at the catalog covered with this year's tagline "The Future Tomorrow." He was sure it was a play on something, other than just being tautologically correct, but he couldn't place it.

Today was opening day, with only three big talks to set the stage and draw in the younger crowd.

The first talk was about the history of star-diving ships, from the first star-diving ship to the current exploration and passenger ships. The speaker also covered the *Hastings* Incident and the subsequent dive rules enforced today, as well as the goal of maps and cartography.

The second talk was on traffic control in dense transit systems. The speaker explained how there was an arbitrary up and down so that ships diving away entered above the line of the dive compared to those arriving below. The ships leaving a jump would report their last star map from that dive to a systems cartography station.

He didn't know the first two presenters, as they were historians rather than researchers. The current and third presenter was Dr. Ryan Marlo, an expert on small-neutron-matter material collection. Marlo droned on about the history of space travel. "For centuries, the stars had been out of reach until humanity got lucky. Then a small amount of neutron star material was discovered in an anomalously heavy comet, much too massive for its size. It was the missing piece in building the prototype ship needed to solar dive. And once the first ship was built, we could go and collect more neutronium. Now, we have an entire industry"—the speaker waved their right hand to encompass the room—

"with dedicated ships to mine neutron stars. Of course, only those that are safe to do so."

Oswald had met him at last year's symposium. The work was needed to keep building the modern gravity drive for the sun ships, thus providing both gravity for the crew and a reaction mass for the gravity drive. Dr. Marlo's talk focused on the changes they were exploring on the cavitation lasers that were used to chip off small pieces of material from far, far, away from the neutron star's surface.

Not knowing who else to meet first, Oswald re-introduced himself at the social hour. "Dr. Marlo, it's been a year. I am Oswald Octavio. I work at the Sky Patrol Cartography Division."

Marlo switched the drink between hands, offering a wet palm for Oswald to shake. "A pleasure. Do you know a Dr. Ron Hayward of Atomic Mining?"

"No, the Science and Regulation departments are both rather large. My particular interests, both professionally and hobby-wise, are the keeping of maps and how they develop."

"Ah, you know who shares your interest? Dillon Eight. He's over there." Marlo gestured with his head. "Looking at the Texel Corporation's poster on space refinements in their new shipping freighters. He runs Eight Transport." Marlo paused. "It was good to speak again, if only for a few minutes.

But I have to get on a call with both my daughter and, more importantly, the committee on the next stage of my funding. Hopefully, you will excuse me. Call me sometime next month, and we can chat." Marlo smiled and bowed slightly as he walked to the elevator.

Oswald sipped his tea and walked over to Dillon Eight and the Texel Corporation salesman. Dillon was taking a pamphlet as Oswald introduced himself.

"Dillon Eight, Dr. Marlo suggested I introduce myself to you. My name is Oswald Octavio of the Sky Patrol Cartography Division."

Dillon swirled his beer and looked down at Oswald. "Okay, hell, I thought you were going to say the Transit Enforcement Division for a second, and my answer to that is, 'I am not my company's enforcement and compliance office.'" Dillon smiled flatly.

Oswald furrowed his brow. "They wear gray like most line officers. Do you get that kind of personal attention often?"

"Not particularly. There was a rather ambitious but clumsy employee of Sky Patrol who thought they could go 'right to the top,' if you will. I was hoping it hadn't become a trend, so I'm pleased it is not. Sometimes you don't know what you're expecting in a conference hall of scientists, salesmen, and Sky Patrol officers. It's probably the giant banners that get me."

Oswald tipped his head slightly. "Well, no, I'm here because it was suggested you share an interest in maps. So, thirty-foot-tall gold, red, and blue banners irritate you?"

Dillon shrugged.

"What did you think of the first talk?" asked Oswald.

"Decent for a mixed-experience audience. I admit I wasn't really paying attention," Dillon answered.

"Not stellar?" Oswald grinned at his pun. "He glossed over why we use 4thprojection maps instead of the 4D-static map."

Dillon shrugged again. "I am familiar with the method, but I leave the 'why' to pilots and historians. So why do we?"

Oswald pulled in a big breath and began, "You know the *Hastings* Incident? Well, a sun ship was lost very early on when second-order dives started being attempted. That's when ships don't go from just one system to another but use a middle star that is gravitationally bridged between two farther stars. The accident, it could have happened in a first-order dive with enough traffic. Generally, when transiting between systems, the transit time is short, a few minutes at worst. Of course, it feels shorter on the ship due to time dilation. With second-order transits, the transit time can be on the order of thirty minutes or more for the research ships going to really far systems on deep gravity wells. Also, when the number of transiting ships starts crowding a star's mapped approach, then the individual gravity wells of the ships start interfering with inbound traffic, so you get the chance that the non-time-adjusted location of the destination has effectively moved or is distorted at your coordinates."

Oswald went on breathlessly, "At this point, we have both issues. At the *Hastings* Incident, it was the first such example. It was on a second-order dive with the *Hastings* going from Alpha Minor to Taurus I, and another ship happened to be transiting the middle star Taurus II to Taurus I at about the same time. It caused the *Hastings* to suffer critical deceleration. And when they exited the dive at Taurus II, the *Hastings* was moving too slowly to escape the sun's pull. It even had a negative velocity in Taurus II's space-time frame. The *Hastings* was pulled back into the sun, right in front of the other ship. The two ships even clipped while passing each other. Fortunately for the surviving ship, the speeds were so fast the bulkheads melted flat like glass where the two ships crossed, rather than having the time to transfer any shock, which would have probably destroyed the ship's integrity." Oswald made a little poof gesture with his hands and continued.

"No ship had been burned up in over a hundred years at that point, so it was an instigating event. The Cartography Division went from being just a part of the Star Science Directorate of Sky Patrol to being paralleled with Transit Coordination. So now every system with a stellar observatory has to use time-projected maps, complete with the ship transit projections for the next three systems that can be reached using a solar dive. Transit Enforcement is still its own division, but it gets all data from Cartography," Oswald finished. He smiled with enthusiasm from sharing his little knowledge nugget.

"Fascinating," Dillon answered. "Are you also a historian?"

"I dabble. I have a small collection of historically printed maps. But there is something about the stars. They have never lost favor in navigation, you know. They're heavenly objects, each one so beautiful. I'm glad humanity can travel amongst them, so we can meet here on Maurus Seven and talk about the future of transport. What did you say your interests were again?"

"Oh, me? Just keeping up with business, you

know. If it helps move goods and services, then I want to be better at it." Dillon offered, "Is there anything in your work you find particularly difficult? I mean, the bureaucracy doesn't stop growing, does it?"

"Never, and sometimes these great investments don't get the attention they deserve. But that's work."

With the lull in Oswald's dissertation in front of his booth, the Texel Corporation salesman cleared his throat and offered Oswald a pamphlet. Oswald glanced at it. "No thank you," he replied.

Dillon inquired, "Do you have a card? I have to excuse myself for a dinner engagement."

Oswald offered up his contact. When Dillon left, Oswald realized it was dinnertime, after all, so he set off to find someone else interesting.

Chapter 4. Fiat Lux

Janet watched the pilot push the dive commit handle forward. She felt as if time had frozen. She knew Mr. Davis had pushed the handle forward, but the world sat still; maybe it did. The gravity felt oppressive, first like it belonged to a too-heavy floor and then uniformly and disconcertingly everywhere. The *Galileo* began the jump. With the faint light of Empty-47 disappearing from view, the world around them also went dark. And for thirty-two seconds, they waited. *This is too long. Why can't I see?* she wondered. The light tore back from the ship in a blinding way, revealing the Merideth-Standly system.

"W-what the fuck?" Captain Helena stuttered.

The bridge members looked around at each other.

"That was . . .unexpected," Janet managed to mutter.

"That was anything but expected. No research dive I've been on was in any way similar. I would like it explained at some point," Helena said, "Now, how is the ship?

"Nominal drive readings," reported the pilot, Mr. Davis.

"Nominal Q-JAY readings," reported Janet.

"Nominal navigation, and beacons up," reported Oren at navigation.

"Nominal structural readings," announced Abigail at ship operations.

When all systems were verified, the captain visibly relaxed. Everything was unharmed and working, but the queer feelings still lingered in Janet's senses. These feelings from transit were unexpected and unexplained.

On the ship intercom, Helena announced, "We have successfully arrived at Merideth-Standly. Thank you for a successful free dive." Janet was looking over the readings. The last visual reading from Empty-47 seemed to be similar to the prior two drone free dives. However, it was very inconclusive due to the black-out experienced in diving. They would have to wait to see what the observation drone visual and other reading back at Empty-47 showed when it transited back in a few hours. Considering all the free-dive parameters had followed their expected paths, she didn't have a ready explanation for the disturbing feelings in transit or why it took longer than expected.

"Captain, the ship *Grainger* of Sky Patrol is on comms for you," chirped Abigail.

"Open," Helena responded.

The screen lit up with a smiling face. "Captain Bernard of *Grainger* to Captain Helena of *Galileo*. I wish to congratulate you on what appears to be a successful endeavor. Your public-safety beacon reads green. Please confirm you won't need our assistance."

"Yes, everything seems as hoped," replied Helena, "and thank you. Confirming that we are not in distress."

"Then I will see you at Main, Captain Helena. From where I've contacted you, you'll be six hours behind us. Captain Bernard out." The screen closed the transmission to show the system in front of them.

"Mr. Davis, please begin transit to Main," Helena commanded.

*

Twenty-eight minutes later, the navigation board lit up, interrupting Oren, who was chatting with Yasmin.

"Captain, I'm getting a message from the Merideth-Standly solar observatory. We are receiving a local gravity map update. It's a priority red update, unexpected. The transit paths for the Merideth-Standly system have shifted."

"Oren, how does the new map compare with the one from our dive?" Yasmin asked.

"The difference I'm seeing is . . . Empty-47 is no longer on the map as a usable gravity well," Oren answered, sitting back, stunned.

Helena turned in her chair to face Janet. "This day is filling with unexplained events. Janet and Yasmin, I would like it if you had some ideas. How do we confirm Empty-47's current state?" asked Helena.

Janet answered, "The fact it is not on the gravity map anymore means it has lost density to the point it cannot be mapped from here. What it means, I do not think we can know yet. In a day or so, we might have enough observations correlated to answer that. Might, but nothing is certain without more direct data, and now it seems we will not get any from the monitor drone we left at Empty." Janet was thinking out loud. "We could free dive back, but diving back seems high-risk. We do not know what happened, where the problem is, or why."

Helena smashed her fist on her console. "I am not—" bang "—under any circumstances—" bang "—free diving this ship—" bang "—again."

Janet leaned back, eyes wide. She stammered, "No, no, Captain. I was not proposing that. The original drone, maybe?" She then offered, "We could set up the drone ship like the prior experiments that did not have measured permanent side effects."

"How long?"

"Three to four hours. Everything is in the launch bay from the survey missions. We have to move the Q-JAY back to its test drone and program the observation routine," answered Janet.

"Do it! I want to know what happened to Empty. Mr. Davis, bring the ship to a full stop. Neutral motion to the system coordinates," Helena demanded.

*

Janet was in the middle of uncoupling parts of the Q-JAY from the drive system when Yasmin broke the silence in the engineering bay. Janet jumped a little; Yasmin had been silent since the bridge.

"I finished updating the observation routine. It's a short, one-minute stay at Empty-47. The drone mass is such that the Q-JAY should recover in that time. What do you think happened?" Yasmin asked.

"I do not know. No good theories yet," Janet answered.

"What if we killed it?" Yasmin asked.

"Do not ruminate. We just need to go measure it and see," Janet said.

"Yeah, sorry, just worrying while I was writing the compensated nav map," Yasmin confessed.

"Honestly, I find it hard to believe anything we did could have an effect. And hoping so too," Janet replied.

"You know, it would be damn good luck for us that we had the only way to get out of a system that loses its gravity well."

"I know where you are going with that. If Empty had gone nova for some reason, the solar observatory would not know for two hours, given the standard rate of mass dispersion. This notice was less than thirty minutes. So how could we have caused it? We are talking about a star here."

"Yeah, I know, Janet. It's a powerful singular object. A miracle of the universe. But they do have an equilibrium. We didn't think that we could burn down whole cities with an atom until we did. I'm just not feeling so good about this."

"So, we go take a look and see." Janet stood up and looked at the disconnected device. "The residual energy is at a point where it can be moved to the drone. So, yeah, let us go see."

*

Just as Janet had sat back down at the bridge station, Helena gave the order. "Okay, Janet, launch the drone." There was an eagerness in her command. The captain wanted answers.

"Launching," Janet answered as the drone exited the *Galileo*. A few minutes later, the drone was in position, spooled up, and free dived in a small burst of light.

"Drone away. Time to return, one minute," Janet said.

Mr. Davis spoke up, "That's unusual. We had a small energy spike. The ship's gravity drive system reported a rapid compensation event right as the drone disappeared."

"Please explain," Captain Helena asked.

"Basically, the drive system had to automatically rebalance the pull on the neutronium core," Davis answered.

"What would cause that?" Helena asked.

Janet had a suspicion, when Davis answered, "It means the local gravity shifted, or a giant gravity wave passed us."

"The Q-JAY does create measurable density

changes, but it should be local and not affect this ship," Janet commented.

The drone reappeared on the view screen.

"Looks like it's melting down out there," Yasmin said.

The screen overlaid measurement readings. They showed the drone was white-hot and was shedding radioactivity. The drone exploded in a brilliant purple fireball. The ship collision alarm blared for a half second while the debris impacted the ship.

"No significant damage, Captain. The debris was very uniform and small," Abigail announced at operations.

"Small miracles," commented Helena.

"The data stream was retrieved. Bringing it up onscreen now," Janet announced.

The view screen lit up with a dull red light. They had returned the drone to the same spot from where they had free dived. All over the visual field, there was a blue glow from the fiery inferno of colliding ions separated at the atomic level. The spectrometer readings lit up across the entire spectrum kicking out infrared, a large amount of deep red and a shower of UV, X-rays. The gravitometer readings showed a flat metric.

"Is that the spectral reading on Empty47?" the captain asked.

"No," Janet answered.

Captain Helena turned in her chair to Janet. "What do you mean, no?"

"It is of the immediate vicinity of the drone. The sensors did not see farther than a few meters. Empty-47 no longer registers on the gravity map because it is not there," Janet stated.

Abigail started laughing quietly with a nervous energy, like the demon who was starting to sing in Janet's mind.

"By the heaven's gods, Empty-47 collapsed when we free dived!" yelled Yasmin.

"What in the universe do you mean it collapsed?" Helena was almost apoplectic as she looked over at Yasmin.

Helena switched her glare to Janet as Janet continued, "I . . . I do not know why it does not exist. We are going to need some time to figure this out. The first look at these readings suggests the star suffered a total expulsion due to excess internal pressure, but I do not know why this happened yet."

"If the radiance of a thousand suns were to burst at once into the sky . . ." Yasmin mumbled.

"What about just one?" Oren replied.

Chapter 5. Forget Me Not

Oswald sat at his desk with a headache for company. It was an average Tuesday in the security department of Sky Patrol's Cartography Division, and it wasn't fun to write reports—even about the Interstellar Cartography and Transport Symposium he had attended three weeks ago. The shelves left of his desk held his replica star globe of the night sky of Five Star Prime, known for its singularly expansive view of the sky at night. He sat opposite a big wall screen that currently showed a view of the cartography display of his home system of Jackson. A sad chair from two occupants of this office some time ago was in the corner for guests. Besides the computer on his desk and the black stylus with golden bars on the end next to it, not much else decorated his office. The beige walls were oppressive. At one time, he had asked about the origin of the office's color. Apparently, they had never been another color in their entire history. The computer sat there with little dots blinking away in the corner, indicating how much time it would take before it closed itself for security reasons. *Hundreds of years of computers and ergonomic studies, and desks are still surprisingly uncomfortable*, he thought.

He picked up a peanut from the mess scattered about his desk one . . . at a time . . . killing . . . time.

A status alert from Cartography's mapping system popped up with a loud clang from his system, surrounded by a bright orange banner: "Immediate Map Change Implemented."

This should be interesting, thought Oswald. These changes happened every so often; however, an unscheduled one was unexpected, and he raised an eyebrow. The explored areas were expected to be stable for the next few years. And near the settled areas, all changes were planned, not immediate.

IMMEDIATE MAP CHANGE

RED – URGENT

Origin:
Solar Observatory Auto
Reporting System

RE: Empty-47 Gravity Well Change

Empty-47 no longer on gravity charts as of 2050808 chart counting time. Reported at Holman, Beridan, and Merideth-Standly solar observatories from active transit updates and confirmed with mapping probe. No incidents reported. Map updates propagating. Final update is expected by 2050837 chart counting time.

He blinked for a minute. That was not just unusual, and not even very interesting, but downright shocking. He pulled up the star chart for Empty-47. It was, as named, devoid of other objects and not marked for any risk profile like binary systems or other near-nova solar systems. There were three event entries: the original mapping entry, a survey of the system twenty years later and its subsequent naming, and a research project being performed by the *Galileo* at chart counting time 2050805. He pulled up the record for the research project.

Title: A Proposal for Transiting Between Systems without the Aid of Solar Diving.

It was a report from Research Division in stellar transit with an approved ship and crew request. Oswald started reading the proposal, and as he read further, his breathing grew shallow. A subsequent search for the transit records showed that *Galileo* was assigned to the project a month ago, and the ship's transit logs and then the lack of them.

This just happened! What the beautiful fuck. That ship wrecked the stars! the thought struck him. He grabbed his stylus from the table, and it felt much heavier than normal. He then selected the record for the proposal, the third line on the Empty-47 update record, the proposal, and the ship *Galileo*, and requested a classification change. His status wall lit up with the face of the vice admiral of Sky Patrol.

"Oswald, what are you playing at?" Vice Admiral Walreed of Sky Patrol asked.

"Sir, I need the heads of Research Division, Cartography Division, and Security for an Archangel classification authorization."

"What could possibly be an Archangel Event out in Cartography?" the vice admiral asked as he keyed in the request.

"I'll explain shortly," Oswald replied.

Three other faces all appeared on the status wall. It looked like Director Masai of Research Division was in his office. Director Lydian of Cartography was backed by the large star map of the charted galactic area. Commodore Logan of Security had his room obscured in black. If they had been in a meeting, they were in this one now.

The vice admiral introduced the meeting. "I can see your security status registers each of you as alone and audio-visually isolated. You all got a level 1 security, AA priority message. These are nearly unheard of. There are only three notification events in that classification category: one, a multi-planet civil war has broken out; two, an Archangel Finding has happened; or, three, an alien incursion is occurring. What we have is a request to classify an event as an Archangel Finding."

The admiral continued, "I'll remind you that invoking this classification means that the cumulative set of items can only be revealed when a multi-planet extinction-scale threat is realized. To my knowledge, that has never occurred. And I couldn't tell you how many Archangel Findings there have been, as they are self-classifying. I won't go through the safeguards to abuse, but needless to say, one of the qualifying criteria to invoke the request was ostensibly realized. Oswald, if you would summarize but not detail the request."

Oswald cleared his throat and began, "Gentlemen, there appears to be an insanely dangerous situation with a recent research experiment. Due to the likely implications, I need Archangel authorized. According to the premise of the Archangel classification, I am requesting that the events I am highlighting on the screen be reclassified. Additionally, I would request to have Dr. Yasmin Invenes and Dr. Janet Avlen, who are listed as lead scientists, both be classified under Archangel; the rest of the crew quarantined; and the research ship destroyed."

The vice admiral prompted, "Maybe a little more detail?"

"Sirs, the sun ship *Galileo* was assigned to a test that involved a novel form of solar diving from Empty-47 to Merideth-Standly. The transit logs show that the ship left for Empty-47 and yet, without a return log, was known to be farther than Main of the Merideth-Standly system at 2050807 chart counting time. The contact time with *Galileo* and the disappearance of the Empty-47 star happened within one chart increment. That is too fast for coincidences."

Cartography clicked Approved and disappeared without a word. Security leaned in and steepled his fingers. The vice admiral leaned back in his chair and blew out a breath.

The head of the Research Division visibly blanched and stated, "You're implying the research here is linked to Empty-47 no longer being mapped?"

"Yes, we know that the gravity drive interacts with the gravity well of a star. Whatever *Galileo*'s mission was, that star, Empty-47, is gone because of it," Oswald said.

"It could be many such reasons. But you may be right in the level of criticality of the risk. I've been following the research, and most of it is classified and not in the report you flagged. However, to help Security make their decision, this wasn't a weapons test. This isn't some agent gone awry, but a failure of risk imagination of the test plan, but it is containable. Conducting the research in an uninhabited system wasn't just for scientific expedience. I'm adding the classified reports to the findings and approving all but the people. A gag order and replacement of history captured by Archangel will be enough. They're qualified scientists, not criminals."

"But, sir, they have all the knowledge to threaten—" Oswald began.

"No. They can't do what they did without help. It's clear from the list of restricted items on the research proposal that they need access to some special parts and materials—parts that even planetary governments don't routinely have. And materials handled in special channels. Between restricted access and the gag order, that should be sufficient," the admiral affirmed.

"I agree with the vice admiral," Security said. "I don't want a watershed moment here. I would hope we have never classified a person under Archangel; it's a death sentence. Although we can probably never know. Still, there's no crime for either of the people you listed."

"A secret of two is only a secret if two are dead," Oswald grumbled.

"The good doctors have security clearances for a reason, Oswald," the director of Security said. "I think we can trust them to withhold the appropriate information. As for the material of that secret, I agree we bury it."

"Regardless, I want this scrubbed into oblivion so that only the last human alive would be allowed to look for options in this file," Oswald answered.

The vice admiral answered, "I wish it really was so easy to bury technology sometimes." He looked at the highlighted report and continued, "What you're showing me here, it's hardly fathomable, but Research agrees with the assessment. I wouldn't trust myself if I had all the pieces, so I am sure as hell not going to let anyone else have them. I'm approving the technology, the gag order, and the ship quarantine, but I will not kill two people for what is probably an accident with no immediate consequences."

"No immediate consequences!" Oswald leaned forward.

"Not to life or irreplaceable history or material, no," was the vice admiral's response.

The head of research shook his head. "This is why we tread lightly. I'm glad the protocols did what they were supposed to do, letting the right people know at the right time. Keep anyone from getting hurt. Do what you need to do with the ship and equipment." He disappeared from the wall.

Security looked up. "Okay, I've got a gag order for the seven weeks prior, *Galileo* ship time, and a quarantine order ready for 'evacuation only: do not board, corpus solum, no equipment, no connect, destroy after evac.' Admiral?"

"Approved. I've granted reclassification of the total technology group and the individual events and event pairings," the vice admiral said. "Any other information, Oswald, that needs to be listed? Once it's gone, you can't request to add it because, well, there's nothing to add it to."

Oswald searched for anything else that needed to be added. He added the ships' communication logs from after their return. "That's it, sir. I pray that the *Galileo* crew stays silent."

The vice admiral nodded. "Commodore Logan, will you conference with me in two minutes on this? We're going to need to put in some handling provisions. Oswald, thank you for flagging this. You no longer have to monitor this." The remaining two section heads and vice admiral disappeared from the screen.

Fifteen seconds later, Oswald watched his computer logs, files, and records of what he had marked vanished from inventory. The Archangel order would be complete in a matter of minutes.

With a fury, he swept the peanuts and other debris from the desk. His jaw tightened as he looked at the cartography display that had returned to his screen. It sparkled back at him. He threw the stylus he still held at the wall, and it banged off the screen harmlessly. His whole body was quaking. *Fuck, what happened out there, Invenes and Avlen, Avlen and Invenes? How could you be so reckless with the stars?*

Chapter 6. Your Eyes Have Their Silence

Janet lay in her bed staring at the ceiling, playing regret me not, pulling little petals off flowers in her imagination as she picked off things that might have gone differently. She had so very far and yet so very little.

Her door chimed. "You look like I feel," Yasmin said as she walked in.

Janet sat up, swinging her feet off the bed. Yasmin sat at the other end of the mattress.

"I imagine I look like the embodiment of someone who just blew up the world, and all I see are ashes," Janet answered.

"Damn, Janet, don't be so cavalier. I'm frightened. I hate this. I wanted to see between the stars, not build . . ." Yasmin sat at the edge of the bed and started crying. Janet reached over, but Yasmin shrugged it off. "Don't touch me."

"I . . . what can I do, Yasmin?"

"You can look at the data."

"I did. Same as you. Everything fit the expected

parameters. Your navigation estimation, my density-to-gravity-well calculations."

"And yet we left absolute destruction behind. That spectral reading from the drone we sent back looked exactly like a nova but colder. You know it, and I know it."

"There is no way to say that was a consequence of the free dive."

"Are you sure? Did we ignore the warnings in the first drone tests?"

"Those came back perfect too. In fact there were no issues at all. The only unexpected phenomenon was the dimming of Empty-47 by a fractional amount of luminosity when we free dove."

"Those tests were done by small mass ships only three times the interdiction line distance from Empty."

"You are the ERC expert. How does that make a difference?"

"I don't know—" Yasmin paused "—I don't know if we can stay partners . . . or friends."

Janet was caught, breathless. She tried reaching out again. "Stop." Yasmin stood up. She slapped her hand over her heart. "I care. I believed. I thought we could take us one step farther across this wonder of stars. With you! Did you secretly know this could happen?"

"No, of course not, Yasmin. I will figure it out. I want to make it right."

"Do you? I don't think you can. Make it right. Are you seriously going to keep trying? I can't be with someone who makes weapons." Yasmin started pacing across the room.

"I don't make weapons. I do science." Janet held her hands out in defense.

Yasmin turned. "Do you? I just saw the most dangerous thing in history unleashed. They say God created the heavens in a day. But now here comes Janet to undo all that."

"That is not fair," Janet retorted.

"To hell with atomic bombs," Yasmin continued, uninterrupted. "Those are playthings by comparison. Vishnu, the destroyer of worlds himself, couldn't do any better! Q-JAY can annihilate an entire star system, and it's got my name all over it!"

"I am not making weapons, Yasmin."

"You don't have to. If Pandora's box was real, you opened up fifty thousand of them."

"I need to know what we did wrong."

"You need to quit. Destroy it."

"I want to close Pandora's box," Janet stood up and pleaded. "It can be closed. I know it."

"That's not how that works. Someone, somewhere will figure out how to break whatever fix you come up with. You didn't listen to a damn thing I just said!"

Janet stared at Yasmin.

"You can't let it go?" Yasmin asked.

Janet shook her head, and Yasmin turned away.

"But . . ." Janet trailed off as the door closed behind Yasmin.

The silence hurt. How much was she going to lose in a day? How many people were going to point their fingers at her? She looked at her data pad, pulled it off her arm, threw it against the wall, and then stomped on it. It shattered.

*

On the bridge, Captain Helena had ordered the second shift to stay quartered; it was not a good time to turn over the bridge crew despite being well past shift change. It had been two hours since the return of the probe. *Galileo* was in transit to Merideth-Standly Main.

Abigail had her head down on the operations desk when it alerted, the indicators lighting her cheeks up amber red. She propped herself up and read the board.

"Captain . . ." Her eyes widened. "The ship, no, this, okay, not okay, there's a failure in the ship's data isolation protocol." She started tapping buttons furiously. "No, no, no, no. Something has been granted access. It's . . . well, shit, that was fast." She looked away from the console to Helena. "We don't have any logs or records." She set her hands back down in resignation. "Or anything!"

Helena was half out of her chair. "What do you mean, anything?"

"I mean, the system has been reduced to its core protected operating instructions that allow the ship to navigate in-system. There's nothing left. And, if I'm not mistaken, the memory core is continuing to write garbage and erase itself at a rate that will cause the core to slag itself in a few minutes. I no longer have any control over the ship besides life support," Abigail answered.

"Confirming, I only have basic navigation," Oren said. "We can't do any solar dives."

Helena slumped back. "Damn, I knew as captain I could do that to the ship. I did not know someone else could."

"Captain, the *Grainger* is hailing us," Abigail interrupted. Helena nodded.

The screen lit up, and Captain Bernard was no longer smiling. "Captain Helena of *Galileo*. I have an order of quarantine from Sky Patrol. You will find your side of communications are blocked. I don't know what has happened. I hope you and the crew are safe. But the order doesn't grant me the privilege of asking what the trouble is. The instructions are that I intercept your ship and disembark your crew. I have also been given navigational command authority of your ship. The rendezvous point is being transmitted to your pilot as a courtesy. I am sorry. Bernard out."

"Abigail, do we have the order?"

"Yes, it came through at the same time as Bernard's message. It is a complete level-one quarantine, full-hazard, do-not-board order. We are the only things to leave the ship, and by only, I mean it specifies we will leave our clothes behind before going between the two airlocks. We have also received an order of silence. It runs seven weeks back and one week forward."

Helena looked at her pad to confirm the delivery of the gag order to their personal pads. All the crew and scientists showed receipt, except Janet.

*

Janet's door chimed. It was the captain. Janet stood up. Helena entered and looked around the room. Janet noticed the captain's acknowledgment of the trashed pad and met her eyes. "Dr. Avlen—"

"Captain, I do not—" Janet interrupted as Captain Helena held up her hand.

"Please do not start with excuses, guesses, or explanations. I don't want to know." Helena paused. "Well, I did, but now we have a gag order."

Janet leaned forward. "And?"

"And I understand and will comply with it. However, I have never been so shocked by something in my whole life. So I can only guess where you may be at," Helena continued. She stiffened and placed her hands palm down in front of her. "Per the order, I advise you not to discuss the incident, the machine, the experiment, that you were on this ship, that you have heard of me outside of an encyclopedia or news article. Do not help put two and two together. Your data and writing from the time on the ship have already been impounded. Well, the whole ship's data set was. It won't surprise me if a great deal of information outside this ship no longer exists."

"Oh." Janet was quiet.

"That said, someday, I wish you to answer the question, 'What the hell went wrong?' before anyone else considers building something like that again. Because I, for one, would never want that repeated. And maybe you'll find answers somewhere. I know you will probably be turning it all over in your mind. But it is clear that you won't have any help." Helena paused and continued, "In the meantime, if you'll forgive me for saying so, it is my extreme desire to forget everything."

Helena turned and left, leaving Janet to slump back on the bed.

***

Janet had seen the training on quarantine protocols but never expected to have to perform one. Her mind was noticing all the little things that are often overlooked in the daily routine, like the plaque on the *Galileo*'s airlock. The beautifully printed ship symbol, registry, and motto, "Purgatory and Truth." The actual off-white of the main walls. The accented gray of the bulkhead and door frames. The red striping of exterior access and the yellow of guides and potential bump injury areas. How crisp the printing on the arrow pointing to the airlock manual lever was—a detail that was only needed when the full triple redundancy of principle ship systems failed.

She was alone in the transfer area. The next crew member was already on the other ship beyond the airlock. They were transferring one at a time. *So quiet*, she heard herself think. As required, she stripped off her uniform, the shoes clopping on the floor and cloth making rubbing sounds. Picking it all up, she looked at the uniform that had been her career for a decade and threw it in the trash. Her tablet that would normally be worn on her arm was already missing, broken in her room. Naked, Janet stood at the entry to the transfer tube.

The airlock was far enough from the working decks of the ship that the gravity from the neutronium core was effectively zero. "Please come forward," a disembodied voice from a speaker resonating through the transfer tube said. Janet floated into the isolation room in the middle of the transfer tether between the two ships. Between the two ships, gravity was equalized between the two neutronium cores.

Exposed out in the tube, knowing that someone was staring just at her, she knew it was their job to make sure she wasn't taking or carrying anything that could not be seen by the CAT and MRI scanners that surrounded the tube. And she knew this was not being recorded, as this was part of the do-not-transfer protocol. She wasn't ashamed of being naked. Janet had visited nude beaches. People occasionally looked and took notice of her physique, and she didn't mind. —Consciously, she knew that the person on the other side of that video monitor didn't know what had happened with her experiment—that she was the only person ever to destroy a star. But she couldn't help feeling that the watcher knew. This was different from those other experiences. She knew all these things but still felt so very exposed. Janet felt shame. She wanted to cover up. Having never been in zero gravity without clothes only added to the over-awareness of sensations. She could feel her breasts acting independently of her chest. Her hair wisped around her back. Even the hair tie was not permitted. Janet shivered. It felt cold even though it wasn't. She blushed and, without thinking, crossed her arm over her chest. The momentum shift started her spinning slightly.

The door to the *Grainger*'s airlock opened, and an airflow blew past. She pulled herself through. The new gown appeared from a shoot as the door closed behind her. She grabbed it and couldn't get it on fast enough. Her leg caught trying to put it through the underwear. Then she had the arm in backward. Then finally, she could get it zipped, only to pinch her stomach, causing her to yelp.

A security guard greeted her when the primary airlock door opened.

"Welcome aboard, Avlen. Unfortunately, we were instructed not to use the overflow quarters, so everyone is being bunked in cargo bay two. You will not have access to any other part of the ship.

We will brief everyone when they are in the bay. I will accompany you on your way," he instructed.

Janet nodded and kicked off a ledge down the hallway. As she passed through the outer decking, gravity returned slightly. The sign for cargo two was three decks down. She landed and found it was at half standard gravity. *Everyone is going to have to ride belted in to whatever our destination is*, she realized. As befitting a recovery vessel, it was a large room with a ceiling two decks high and low-gravity chairs for the occupants.

Half of the occupants of *Galileo*'s former crew sat around staring at their knees like prisoners. Yasmin was picking at her arm. She glanced at Janet with abandonment in her eyes and went back to twisting the skin on her left arm.

It took forty more minutes to get the rest of the crew transferred. The speaker system announced, "I am Captain Bernard of *Grainger*. I hope we can make your stay reasonable for being assigned to the cargo bay. This announcement provides some guidelines and information for the journey. The belts are for your safety, of course. The ship cannot fully compensate for acceleration at this deck level. Daslet facilities are available at the bulkhead door right of the entrance door. Please do not congregate.

I cannot permit it at this time. My instructions are to take you to Merideth-Standly orbital transfer station. It is about an eight-hour ride. There, you will be held in detention for two days, when the processing specialist is expected to arrive."

A groaning was heard across the cargo area. "Per the orders given, I cannot answer any more questions. Nor will I hear any plea. I will be forced to isolate anyone who violates any of the orders they have received. I am very sorry." The intercom went quiet.

Janet glanced around at the other refugees. No one paid her any mind except Oren, who was spaced a chair away. He smiled and gave a double thumbs-up. "Just like navigating the stars, navigate the process, Janet." He returned his gaze forward, apparently to meditate. She slumped down in her bucket chair and felt so very alone again.

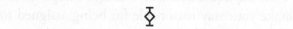

Chapter 7. Let the Dawn Not Blind You

Janet didn't know about Yasmin or the others. She had been separated on arrival at Main and taken to a detention wing. With no view of the hallway, she did not know who came or went. A light port on the rear wall provided a good simulation of the outside to avoid this being an "isolation" room and giving the feeling of being absolutely trapped. The cell was otherwise an inoffensive off-white with a rather large sixteen-by-eight footprint. A bunk bed and a small table shared this side of the divider to the daslet. It had been longer than the promised two days before the man, now sitting at a portable desk propped across the width of the cell door, had arrived.

"Please," he offered, gesturing to her side of the desk

She moved the stool in her cell to the desk, and he continued.

"Obviously, you have already been processed per quarantine orders when you were taken onboard the *Grainger*. Have you read the entirety of the silence order provided to you?"

"Yes," answered Janet. It had been handed to her on hard copy when she had been given her cell. She suspected everyone else had been given simpler electronic copies due to the rather lengthy and specific stipulations to material handling that pertained to her research in the silence order. She looked over his dark green security uniform. It was decorated with the *psi* of psychology on the shield of security. *Security division psychology specialist, that is disconcerting*, Janet thought.

"Have you read the addendum?" the man asked.

"It was four hundred pages long," Janet replied.

"Four hundred and thirty-two. Then you have read it?" he persisted.

She had read it. It had taken three extra days for her processing person to arrive. She had plenty of time to read it.

"Yes," she replied.

"Okay, may I ask you some questions?" he started.

Janet waited. They stared at each other for a minute.

"Thank you," he said, and leaned back, steepling his hands.

"You didn't ask anything," Janet said.

"I did. You didn't respond. Can you tell me about the day after your dissertation defense?" he asked.

That caught Janet off guard, although she was relieved to talk to someone about something—and on any other topic than her reason for being in this cell. Being cooped up and alone for five days, even with a synthetic window, was pushing her mind sideways.

"I had a small dinner party with my colleagues, adviser, and a few faculty of the research institute. They gave me a book on the history of physics. I spent the day earlier filing my graduation paperwork and preparing for my move to the research institute on Novus."

"Were you happy?"

"Ecstatic."

"Were you in love at the time?" he asked.

"What does that—" Janet started.

"Please just answer."

"No, I was rather heartbroken, actually. I was ready to move on."

"How about now?"

"I cannot answer that question," Janet stared at him, stone-faced.

"Correct, you can't."

He reached down to his bag, produced a piece of paper followed shortly after by a pen, and put them on the desk. The paper was a blank except for a glittering blue border with a snake weaving around the perimeter that indicated a Sky Patrol judgment order.

"Paper?" Janet asked.

"Please sign here." He pointed to the lower left part of the page.

"It is blank," she protested.

"Yes. As you know, Sky Patrol is one of the guarantors of your signature; the other is your Enderhall certificate. If you were to sign an electronic file, it could not be altered afterward to suit the needs of whatever Sky Patrol needed you to agree to."

"I think not," Janet said.

"Okay," and he stared at her.

"Is that how I get out of here?"

"No. You can leave in about an hour from now," he replied. "However, here is a choice. You may sign the paper, and Sky Patrol will place you at Maiman-Hall Research Institute. There, they study laser-magnetic-semiconductor interactions and devices. You have the fundamentals. Work there for a minimum of three years, and you may transfer to many other places. However, your personnel record shows you are banned from handling several technologies, so do expect some limits. If you don't sign it, you will no longer be employed with the Sky Patrol Research Directorate or Sky Patrol in any capacity, nor will you be allowed to rejoin Sky Patrol of your own accord. You are, of course, free to find your choice of employ."

"Of course," she said.

"Of course," he fawned.

"What goes on the paper?" she asked.

"I don't know."

"Where—"

"I don't know."

"How many times have you given someone a blank piece of paper to sign?" Janet said.

"Three. Two of them today. I will leave the paper and the pen here with you. As I said, they will release you in an hour," and he got up to leave.

"How is Yasmin?" Janet asked as he stood to go.

"You may find out when you are released," and he left.

The security ward waited for her to take the paper and pen and then picked the table out of her doorway before shutting the door. As promised, after an hour, the ward brought plain clothes, replacement shoes, and a new electronic pad for her. She slipped on the clothes, snapped the pad to her arm holder, and went to the facility lobby, where she tore the paper, wadded it up, and threw it and the pen in the trash.

Examining the pad: her travel plans were blank, her Sky Patrol employment was terminated eight weeks ago, and her current employment was blank. That was it then.

What now? What do you do when you have all the choices in the galaxy and no plans? she thought.

She slumped against the nearest wall and slid down. Whatever had cleaned up her history had done so thoroughly. She had to search for "Yasmin Invenes, doctor, Persius colony" to find her connection ID on the new pad.

Janet clicked call, but it shunted, and Janet got an auto-reply.

We died among the stars.

Janet stayed there long enough for her eyes to clear. Heaving herself off the ground, she thought, *Step two, go find some food.*

*

The fries grew cold in front of her. She had enjoyed the hamburger, but she couldn't keep eating just for pleasure. Janet stared out across the food court. The location was mostly empty this afternoon. A few other Sky Patrol members of ambiguous officers sat in their gray uniforms. Another in blue walked with a plain-clothes person.

She scrolled through her pad, looking at her work history. It had been changed too. School was the same, but she had a new dissertation she didn't write.

She pulled the pad off her arm. *Home. Pick a transit route.* A few hundred popped up on the display. *So many. Oh, my constraints are reset.* She tapped at the pad. *Let's hope all the rest of my life isn't going to be a series of small decisions made momentous now,* she thought wearily. She set down the pad.

Okay, definitely home first. Settle my thoughts. Find somewhere to work. Then what? Then what . . . ? An idea popped into her mind, and Janet picked up the pad and looked at it. Video message:

> *Hi, Vilnus. Sorry I have been out of touch lately. How is your trip so far? Anyway, would you like to come to Horizon Four with me? I have a serious problem. I cannot talk about it, but I would appreciate the company. I am feeling lonely out here.*

Chapter 8. Unstoppable Shield
– Immovable Spear

Oswald sat in his chair, staring at the ceiling. It was a Wednesday. The Psychology Shield summary was on his desk display. He didn't have the full report, as he didn't have need-to-know access. It wasn't important to his purposes anyway.

Overview

The general crew of the sun ship Galileo are all expected to fully comply with the silence order. The senior officers are expected to regard the silence order with all due seriousness.

Captain Helena fully understands the implications of violation. Combined with her excellent record, it is recommended she retain command.

Dr. Invenes is expected to comply with the silence order, at least consciously. Sub-consciously she may begin expressing distress and unwittingly convey information about the time period in question. She will require continued psychiatric intervention. She signed the open paper.

Dr. Avlen will comply with the silence order and is currently stable. She may seek to absolve herself of doubts about the time in question. It is assumed that restrictions on her access to listed technologies will be sufficient. She did not sign the open paper and has resigned from Sky Patrol.

With the report was a redacted message Dr. Invenes had sent to her physiatrist. Normally those messages were locked, but just enough restricted keywords meant the Psychology Shield tracking order was allowed to open it and analyze the flagged paragraph. Without being a member of Psychology Shield, he only had the analysis. Therapists were confidential, but this is how rumors spread—rumors he didn't want to be thought of as true.

Dr. Invenes's message indicated that she was

indeed clearly worried: worried about the implications of the "recent event" and that the government
would be suppressing the "recent event" rather than
warning of the dangers.

Oswald had a scheduled meeting with the director
of Security, Commodore Logan. He anticipated the
director had not gone far enough and that it was his
duty to keep up the pressure.

Logan appeared on the wall display opposite
Oswald's desk. "Oswald, is there a concern?"

"Yes, one of the scientists is showing signs of
breaking the silence order."

"Oh?"

"Yes, Dr. Invenes is writing 'help me' letters to
her psychiatrist."

"As well she might, Oswald. She was under a lot
of stress from whatever happened." He waved his
hand as if waving off a fly. "We sent her through
a quarantine run, and now she is under a lifelong
gag order. Tell me you might not need to want to
talk it out, even if hyperbolically?" Logan asked.

"This is not the kind of thing one should really
ever talk about."

"Like we are talking about now? Let it rest. This
is why we have Psychology Shield. Don't keep
opening cans of worms that you want to leave
sleeping," the commodore answered.

Oswald squinted in reaction. "Sir, would you reconsider your decision on a capital outcome?"

"About what, Oswald? There is no crime to charge her. There are no records of any malfeasance, no records of any kind. I don't know what she's been up to, and I cannot ask her. I believe that was the intent of the classification meeting. We have trials, even closed ones, for capital determinations, even terrorists and insurrectionists, Oswald."

"We don't need a trial. She signed the open paper."

"Would you sign one?"

"No, I—"

"No, you wouldn't. And she did. Do you realize what level of trust that means she has placed in us? We owe her that same level of respect. And I really expect you to leave this alone," Logan replied.

"And of Dr. Avlen?"

"What of her? She is rather restricted in her own way. Oswald. Look, I'm going to send over a Phycology Shield counselor. Not mandatory you keep seeing them. A courtesy for any stress you have been under. I have my own therapist I talk to every three months for several hours to work out conflicts I run across. Or if you think you need to be re-evaluated for your responsibilities?"

"No . . . no, I am fine, sir."

"Okay. Consider it if you need. We are here to

help. And Psychology Shield will keep an ear out. You did your job. Please, no more talk of taking action for things that—" Logan waved out both hands as if waving a baseball runner safe "—never . . . happened, Oswald."

"Okay. Well, thank you for the time."

"Anytime." The commodore smiled and closed the connection.

What you don't take care of today are tomorrow's regrets, Oswald thought. He regretted not being able to be more drastic with the gag order request. *What are two people compared to possibly saving millions?* But it wasn't his decision, ultimately. Wishing into the ceiling, Oswald realized, *I don't have the authority level I need. I don't even have a way to get it from someone who could act.*

He leaned back in his chair and blew his breath out. He wondered if that was a threat or a genuine offer to help from the commodore. Just as bad either way. He needed to stay vigilant where he was and keep watching, his own little searches running in the background. The ceiling was almost interesting now.

*

Three hours later, the computer popped up another tracking alert. *What now?* Oswald moved to look at his desk screen. *Another Invenes problem?* he wondered.

Dr. Avlen to visit Horizon 4.

Her transit was scheduled for seven weeks. The details of the Horizon system came with the notice. The cartographic listing gave Horizon as a system with five planets and two asteroid belts. It was a mostly uninteresting system with some minor asteroid mining on Horizon 2 and Gaetan Research Institute on Horizon 4.

He rapped his finger on his desk. *What is at Gaetan Research?* he asked the computer. The list of seven researchers, ten assistant researchers, a list of publications, and their specializations came on screen. The research institute was built to study the tidal interactions between the asteroids and the star, which demonstrated unique gravitational interactions. The research center was more than just a building. There was a class VII research vessel assigned to the institute and equipped with two full-system radar monitoring sets. *Overkill?* he thought as he kept reading. Oswald leaned in, peering at the listing, trying to divine why this notice was sent. None of the exact issue words had popped up in the tracker alert, so what weird combination made the tracker flag this visit, he wondered.

Browsing the titles of the recent papers, two stood out: "Gravitational Nonlinear Shifts in Orbital Motion," and "Asteroid Rogue Bodies Escaping a Chaotic Attractor." Opening the abstracts, he read each.

"This reads like Invenes's research. Shit, shit, shit, are you fucking damn kidding me? I bet you feel guilty, but leave this alone," he cursed to the room.

Getting up, he began pacing around the office. *Damn these martyrs*, Oswald thought. *What does it take to keep the stars safe from you sons of bitches?*

He didn't know how long he had been pacing when the communication link rang for his attention. He stared at it furiously. He tapped it, voice only.

"Oswald here," he answered curtly.

"Hey, Oswald, this is Dillon. We met at the cartography conference a few months back."

"It's a terrible time, Dillon. I'll have to call you back."

"Do you believe in serendipity?"

"What?"

"Do you believe in serendipity?"

"Not particularly. Sometimes things just happen in a succession that feels like good or bad fortune. But it's just coincidence," Oswald reassured himself, even though he was really having a very bad day at this point and wondering what cosmic joke was being played on him at this moment.

"Well, I have your card, and I have a star question," Dillon persisted.

"Fine, make it short."

"Well, my ships can't transit through Empty-47 anymore, and—"

"Shut up, shut up now!" Oswald screamed. "By all the galactic orders I can issue you, shut up now!"

"Okay . . ." Dillon paused.

"What, what would you even talk about that place for?" Oswald demanded.

"Well, as a large shipping firm, I found a discrepancy pop up for a quad jump route, and I thought I would ask you."

"Why me?" Oswald asked.

"I have your card. You said you liked maps. You're in the place that manages solar cartography. Remember what I said Sky Patrol did with me, with their enforcement officer coming to me directly? So why go beating up and down the bureaucracy to get answers?" Dillon responded.

That was a shitty excuse, thought Oswald, *Quad jump. No one uses quad jump routes besides Transit Research.*

"No, I don't think . . ." Oswald started. "You smuggle, don't you." It wasn't a question.

"Eight Transport moves goods and services efficiently, my friend. We ship general goods. And we have an asteroid-mining division and metal-transport division that specializes in the heavies, ruthenium, quarent, and such. So can you help me?" Dillon answered coldly and then perked up, "Do you need something shipped?"

"Shipped my ass. Why would I need something shipped? Oh, never mind. If you have something other than stupid questions that I won't answer, then call me later when it's interesting, okay?" Oswald answered.

"Yeah, sure. Finding how to improve the lost time would improve the lives of many. But as you ask, I'll call you back another—"

"Wait! Maybe I do need something shipped. If we meet, would you be able to handle some small animals, that are quite precious, for a friend? Maybe I can tell you how we handle our maps to fix the lost route?"

"We can ship almost anything to anywhere, Oswald."

"Be at your office five days from now. I will come to you," Oswald said and hung up. He pulled the pad off his arm, pulled up the scheduled transit to Eight headquarters, and booked himself personal transit.

$\diamond$

Chapter 9. Tell Me About Tomorrow

Janet glanced over at Vilnus, who was strapped in the chair next to her. They were on the transport rocket, taking them to the sun ship 238-Bonet, which would ultimately take them to Horizon 4.

"You did not have to come on this trip. I appreciate you being with me," Janet said.

Vilnus smiled back. "Oh, I know, but I like to get out of my office occasionally. They painted it a really dreadful color of gray-blue a couple of years ago. Plus, you know, I enjoy exploring new science even when I'm not sure what I am going to see. You can piece together some interesting new things doing that. Horizon has been on my list for a little while after I saw the research they are doing on the double asteroid ring. And you asked."

Janet smiled back.

"So why are you going here?" Vilnus asked.

"Maybe I like getting out of the office too."

"I doubt it. Your office looked out on an ocean."

"Just a lake. Unfortunately, it no longer does."

"What do you think you will do next, now that you quit the Research Directorate?"

"I do not know. I really do not, and it terrifies me."

"Well, there are a lot of options. A whole galaxy's worth. Maybe it would be easier to decide what you don't want to do. Then the list might be more constrained," Vilnus offered. "So why this trip?"

"As you said, exploring my options. I am interested in Dr. Harrison's gravity research," Janet said.

"Ah, yes. But you're an expert already. You were going to defeat the sun's pull." Vilnus gently pulled his fists apart in a spray of fingers.

Janet winced. "Please do not talk about that. I cannot and will not talk about it. And it makes me uncomfortable."

"Sorry, I didn't realize. Okay, so what is Dr. Harrison's research about?" Vilnus asked.

"Well, as you are about to discover, I am interested in his multi-body gravity work. It is focused on the asteroids, but I expect it can be used for something else. So I thought an in-person dialogue would be nice," Janet answered.

"Should be interesting," Vilnus agreed. "Reminds me, have you considered Texel Corporation? They work on gravity drives."

"I really have not. I know they build a lot of the drives. Would it be interesting?"

"Well, a few months ago, I got to see some of the research they were collaborating on at Linus. It would seem they have an extensive research arm. You would already be familiar with the fundamentals. I mean, you bragged about personally taking apart the gravity lace."

"I thought they just did production. They are not one of the groups that farm out all their development to some other company?"

"I'm sure they do some of that too. It's just that you're used to working for a large organization. You might find it familiar. And if you don't like working for that group, move to another, or change companies."

Janet frowned.

"I know, you want to pick the best path from the start, and you like and expect to succeed with perseverance. That's not always possible. I'm just saying, now that you are changing paths, embrace the ability to change. Don't identify with what you do, but with success."

"Sounds like you should go on a speaking tour. Have you been forced to a new career path?" Janet retorted.

"Not forced, no, but you know I was pretty unhappy in the last year at my prior position. I could have stuck with it and probably done shoddy work, but it was better I try something new. I even got a new role recently with Sky Patrol just before my last Five Star trip. It can be easier to change your career and what you do the second time. But I get this"—Vilnus waved to encompass the transport bay—"change isn't easy at all. It's really a total change in your identity. You were your work. Now, you're you, looking for something new."

"True," Janet answered. "Hope I find it soon. Tell me about your last trip to Five Star Prime?"

Vilnus smiled and began describing his favorite arboretum there. They had built twenty-foot-tall shrubbery shaped like a variety of animals, such as rabbits, wolves, and grandos, all made from an array of different flowers and bushes.

***

The solar dive had taken two jumps and twenty hours of in-system navigation to reorient to where Horizon 4 was in orbit relative to their dive end point and get around the asteroid belts safely. Janet, with Vilnus, was strapped into two of the sixteen seats that were arranged in two rows on either side of the small ship that was their surface transport. The small ship could land, launch itself, and fly inter-atmosphere to get around the planet. These

ships were used in systems that didn't have transport infrastructure.

Horizon 4 was now visible on their seat view
screens. "Vilnus, Janet, we land in fifteen minutes,"
Andre, the drop ship pilot, announced.

As they were landing, Janet could see the far-off
hills and vast stretch of plains-land grass and inter-
mittent dry patches that led to where the research
center was located. The grass was yellow-beige this
time of year. The center itself was on the edge of
a small wash. Beyond the center, the grassland
continued further.

A clear area was around the front of the center.
They landed a few hundred meters away. Janet
and Vilnus stepped out into fairly cool weather.
A smiling middle-aged man was walking toward
them with his hand up in greeting.

"Welcome to Gaetan Research Institute. I'm
John. If you wouldn't mind letting me check your
identification before I take you in?"

Janet, Vilnus, and their pilot Andrew produced
their arm tablets' identification screens. John looked
at them briefly and beamed a smile, gesturing them
to follow.

"This way, please. We are glad you could visit.
I'm a research fellow here. It's a joy when we can

share the sights and insights we get to discover in this unusual system."

Vilnus took in the landscape. He walked a little sideways to run his hand over the grass that lined their path.

"How long have you been here?" Janet asked.

"From the beginning. I helped Harry get the project started. My research has always been in tidal body motion, and you are about to learn how unique this system is."

As he proceeded inside, Vilnus's eyes opened at the open sky foyer, drenching the interior in natural light.

"Dr. Harrison will be out briefly. The conference room is over here." John pointed to his left. "We just got done with the daily out-brief, so there are donuts if you want them. Tea, Pavojų Fruit, sugar soda?" John asked as he walked them to the room.

Janet took a Pavojų Fruit drink. "Soda, please," Vilnus replied as they sat down in the room. The room's ten chairs were lined along a black table whose rectangular surface narrowed at one end. Vilnus noted the edges of the desk were beveled inward as he ran his hands on it when he sat. The chairs were midcentury reproductions. He turned and looked through the large exterior window that was framed with the same black glass material as the tabletop. It looked out on the prairie, which was covered in long grass that waved gently in the wind.

"I see you like the view?" Dr. Harrison said as he walked in the door.

Janet answered, "It is lovely. I am Dr. Avlen, and this is Dr. Boren. We go by Janet and Vilnus."

"Dr. Harrison, call me Harry. I'm the lead researcher," he said, extending his hand. "I am glad you could make it to our lovely institute. Hopefully you'll both take away some unique perspectives to your respective institutes. To answer the unasked question, the grass is a local variety found mostly in the northern hemisphere. Interestingly, not much fauna has adapted to this part of the planet. We assume the biosphere here is only a few tens of million years old is why."

"Is that why the asteroids are unique in this system, because it is young?" asked Janet.

"Or why the planet's biome is young. Asteroid impacts set it back. Because the uranium decay measurements make this planet about two billion years old," Harrison replied. "Janet, you arranged the visit, so I'll ask Vilnus first. Is there anyone here or anything in particular you wish to see while Dr. Avlen and I talk?"

"Thank you. Not in particular. I am mostly collecting impressions and learning if I might help others at this point."

"Well, Dr. Avlen, in your visit request, you didn't say what you were interested in. I assume since you wanted to talk to me specifically and your prior research has been in improving sun-planet closing-distance time of solar dives, then you are here about my gravity research," Dr. Harrison opened.

"Yes, I am." Janet noted the subtle quoted change in her research history. "I am familiar with the math models for how a sun trades energy with its local environment, electromagnetic, radiation pressure, and gravity. Not just the sun imparting all its energy expenditure on the surrounding system. But your latest paper on how the local asteroids appear synergistic with the sun's energy density proved particularly interesting reading. I was hoping to work out with you modifications that would be required if a high-energy object, on the order of a small planet, was rapidly introduced to a local solar system."

"Oh, that sounds like a challenge. You've just asked if I can extend the asteroid resonance model to one of a more concentrated scale. I can't imagine a scenario when that could happen, but that doesn't mean the universe can't invent one. Let me pull up the model, and we can talk it over."

A large model of the Horizon system appeared on the conference room screen on the end wall. A series of arrows pointed between the sun and asteroids that were looped around and on top of the ecliptic. Harrison pulled up the equation set for the first arrow.

"The model I have so far explores part of ERC theory where the mass of an in-system object's gravity field interacts with the star in the system. The basic theory is Newtonian, original general relativity handled the time dilation within the strong gravity well. ERC did away with any need for the extra constant of general relativity by showing the deep-well coupling was the mechanism by which it looked like there was extra mass in the universe from long-range Newtonian deviations."

"Standard model. What is the part you having been diving into that is atypical here?" Janet replied.

"Okay, so the original system survey listed two asteroid belts and two planets. Typical, except they sent an unusual diagram to the lab I was at. It was unusual enough I was able to, along with John Armstrong, who you met, petition Sky Patrol for this facility twenty-three years ago. Take a longer look at the diagram. Let me remove the arrows."

Janet stared at the diagram for a minute and pointed at the second asteroid belt. "That is wrong. For half the orbit they loop out of the ecliptic without passing a very massive orbiting planet. There should not be a three-body interaction."

"And that is what we came to study. The two asteroid belts are Horizon 1 and 3 broken to bits. The inner belt shows a time dilation effect in its orbit. A very small one, but after tagging many of the asteroids, we could measure it using our research ship, the *Hooke*, and the orbital observation sensors on the far side of the system. But this," Harrison pointed, "the second belt, it is following a chaotic strange attractor. Looks like a three-body problem because it is: it's its own chaotic attractor."

"I have never heard of such a thing," Janet said. "All sorts of objects show chaotic motion, including asteroid individual orbits around the primary orbital path. But that is a standard Newtonian orbit."

"That's why the lab was started. Absolutely new phenomenon. The short version is, there is a shock wave traveling in the orbit of the asteroids. It causes a large amount of the rocks to congregate in one part of the orbit, which creates a large local mass density. The density wave is moving faster than the asteroids individually, so in their relative frame, it is as if the asteroids are performing an out-of-elliptic gravity turn. The asteroids on the opposite side of the elliptical orbit are deflected back around the L3 Lagrange point and reset in orbit in the ecliptic. Horizon 2 and 4 help slow or advance the attractor, so the whole motion is chaotic but stable."

"Weird, and I am going to love it. Let's start with the arrows in your equations that show the ERC approach." The doctor began walking Janet through the equations. Vilnus was only cursorily interested and pulled off his arm pad and went to work reading reports, intermittently staring out the window at the grass and taking short walks. Hours later, they wrapped up.

John showed up with two new pavojų fruits for them. "Do you wish to walk and talk, or shall I just point you in the direction of quarters?"

"Thank you. Point please. I am talked out of being pleasant tonight," Janet said. John smiled and pointed upstairs and to the left. Vilnus headed off with Janet for guest quarters.

"My brain hurts," Janet said as they walked along. "I understand what he is trying to do, but I am not sure he is thinking large enough. His model has all the asteroid coupling modes, but it relies on perturbation theory. I think tomorrow, I'll have to break that assumption so we can get past the linear interpretation into a non-linear model."

"Sounds reasonable. I just like the grass. It's pretty. I found a research assistant here who will show me the grounds tomorrow when we have more daylight."

"Is she attractive?" Janet teased.

Vilnus smirked. "You never know who you're going to meet."

"Yes, and you like your boondoggles," Janet prodded again.

"Hell yes, I like learning outside my discipline. A couple of times, I've solved issues with how to build something, in a radically simpler way, with someone else's tools. Big fan of process improvement," Vilnus answered.

"Great. I'll see you in the morning then," Janet said, and stepped into her room.

***

Morning came, and Vilnus found himself with Avery, who was starting her postgraduate research at the institute. They stood in the landing bay for the institute's shuttle, a half-moon crescent room with a movable canopy several hundred feet above them.

A large portion of sun ship exterior hull was off to the side in a covered maintenance alcove. The alcove was of almost equal size to the landing bay but smaller in height. Working on the side of the ship section were a robot and two other researchers.

Vilnus commented, "That looks like it has an incredible amount of instrumentation in there. I assume it's down here for overhaul; otherwise, you wouldn't want to screw up the calibration with the local gravity?"

"Yes, it's the lower long-range radar array for the *Hooke*, our research ship. It malfunctioned a few weeks back. In an odd way, too, we couldn't use the auto-diagnostic robots to fix it. Fortunately, an upgrade was planned, so we took the opportunity to bring it down. Two weeks more, and we will have it back with the rest of the ship," Avery answered.

"I don't see your surface shuttle down here?"

"Our landing craft is up with the ship," Avery stated.

"Is your research ship the extent of the measurement equipment?"

"Half of it. Harrison probably mentioned the large-area sensor platform orbiting on the other side of the system. But as you guessed, the *Hooke* is packed with sensors, and we get the benefit of moving it to any observation position. Down here is mainly housing, as our ship isn't geared for a long-term crew. We also house the computer systems. There is a second one of those radar arrays aboard ship. Between that and all the other sensors, the ship, even as a class VII research vessel, would be out of room and power for a large crew and the computers. Would you like to see the radar set closer?"

They went over to the maintenance area. Vilnus looked up at the shell of the ship, towering ten times his height. It was one thing to be inside a sun ship and another to be standing next to even a part of one.

Avery gestured at the radar. "Here, you can see how the lower section is wrapped with a multi-frequency radar system and multiple gravimetric sensors."

Vilnus took a moment to lean on the nearby computer console as if to recline. He pulled his Patrol Medallion, the little gray disk of responsibility from Sky Patrol, from his pocket. Pressing it onto the side of the console, Vilnus counted to four in his head and repocketed it.

"There are telescopes on the central band of the ship. As I mentioned, we brought this part of the hull down because, in addition to the repair, we're taking the opportunity to add a complete band of terahertz and infrared radar sensors and a second set of higher-sensitivity gravimetric sensors. Too many parts to do in space without a space dock.

Faster here than getting in the queue at the closest fleet yard," Avery explained.

"What's on the other radar suite?" Vilnus asked.

"Same thing but geared for close-range higher timing sensitivity rather than long-range position sensitivity. Unfortunately, it glitched shortly after this array. It is still partly working, though. We assume that a power feedback issue was at fault. Won't know until it is also down here for repair. The tech experts are tied up on this one," Avery answered.

Vilnus took a pause, glanced at his arm pad, and tapped the new little amber triangle to see the audit summary from the medallion. What he was authorized to see of the audit was not surprising. Flagged as a watch was something wrong with the telemetry data the ship was sending back, just as Avery suggested. Even with the ship's much smaller radar patches, the data seemed incomplete rather than less detailed. The health data from the lower array, before it failed, wasn't accurate either, with integrity checks failing half the time.

"Have you looked at the embedded computer systems in the arrays and communications?"

"No, we just got the sensor down here two days ago, and we don't have the codes to break into their programming when they're installed."

"What are you using to do the research and monitor the asteroids in the meantime?" Vilnus asked.

Avery shrugged. "The research is stalled on this side of the system. The platform on the other side of the system only reports on that side."

"Any safety concerns?"

"Shouldn't be. The planet cleared its path of asteroids, and while the individual asteroid paths are chaotic, they're confined to a recurring pattern. And we expect the asteroid miners would have the courtesy to give us notice if they saw something dangerous. It's lunch. Would you care to rejoin your colleague?"

*

Vilnus stood just outside the conference room door. He closed the report on his arm pad. It had not been any more illuminating than when he glanced at it downstairs. Feeling puzzled, he walked into the conference room.

"So, have you two worked out your mathematical grievances?" Vilnus joked.

"Oh, I think so. The use of perturbation theory was, in some ways, a crutch—an expedience for working with small bodies. When a macroscopic body is used, we have to include three extra resonance terms. Really interesting," Dr.

Harrison answered. "Did you enjoy your tour of the grounds?"

"Good, yes, fascinating. I like the way the institute is constructed. It's Nevinant Collaborative, I believe. I'm a fan of the architectural style. I also saw the research ship's sensor shell. Or at least part of it. I think I am going to take in more of the view while you continue your work." Vilnus sat down and turned to the view outside while Janet and Harrison continued their discussions.

As he looked out at the prairie, the mountains were too far to be seen on the horizon, just the grass stretching over the curvature of the planet and their shuttle sitting a few hundred meters out. Not much in the way of clouds right now. When they had walked in the day before, he had seen some isolated damp spots on the ground from rain that had occurred a few days prior. Through the sunlit window, he watched as the grass swayed in the wind when a puff rose on the horizon. Then the earth shifted under them.

Chapter 10. Over The Horizon Tonight

"Dr. Harrison, is there geologic activity near here?" Vilnus asked, not turning from the window of the conference room.

"No, not particularly. The nearest volcano is seven hundred kilometers away, give or take, and only shallow earthquakes in this part of the continent. It's why we—"

The grass flattened.

Dr. Harrison was drowned out by the violent shudder of the walls of the room. The glass formed a corner crack, and the unoccupied chairs shifted.

Vilnus stood up. As the grass started to rise up again, he saw another puff closer but much smaller. The grass near that blew over for a few hundred meters. Another puff a few kilometers away. It was like little pebbles landing in a sea, a sea of grass. He went pale, and his eyes widened. "Oh, shit. Bad."

"Vilnus, what—" Janet started, and looked right at him, her eyes wide.

Vilnus yelled into his pad, "Andre, we need to

be flying. Emergency. Dr. Harrison, signal a total ground evac!" He started around the table, banging his leg on the edge. The impact barely registered in his mind, full adrenaline setting in.

"May I ask—" the doctor sounded aggrieved.

"No. Hit the alert. Highest level!" Vilnus exclaimed.

"Our only lifter is up with the ship," Dr. Harrison stammered.

The grass blew over and stayed bent. Then the glass shattered.

"Our shuttle is *the* evac point. Get them started!" Vilnus blurted as he grabbed Janet's arm, pulling her from the chair.

"But what—" Janet started.

"The area is being pelted by meteorites. We have minutes. If that. Janet, ship, now!" Vilnus nearly pulled Janet off her feet as he headed out the door.

Janet ran after Vilnus, Dr. Harrison hot on their heels. The alarms were blaring in the building. It was a whirlwind of color: red, green, and orange, no blue. Not medical. Vilnus couldn't think beyond that, with all his energy in his legs. He blasted through the front doors. The ship, so close. He was a quarter way there when he heard and felt the whump of air blowing him sideways off his feet mid-stride, like a blade of grass.

Dust was everywhere. He looked back. Janet was fumbling with Dr. Harrison, pulling him up from the ground. She had a cut on her head, probably from the shattering window. The dust blew past and was replaced by small pebbles born on the ferocious wind. Just a few tens of meters left to the ship. It still sat serenely on the landing pad, half covered in dust. But the ship itself was no shelter, just the ride.

The researchers were streaming out of the complex now. He saw Andre in the middle of the pack but gaining ground. Vilnus turned and continued his sprint. He hurt. His side and throat hurt from running, his leg hurt from the table, and he was tearing up with the incessant dust, eyes blurry when he hit the side of the ship and pulled the hatch open. He wanted to shout that they all hurry. But it was an unnecessary warning. He could see that anyone who had stopped to grab something had dropped whatever they carried, with items littering the path to the compound, in a full sprint to the ship.

Andre came running up, right through the hatch. Vilnus pushed Janet through, followed by Harrison.

"How many?" wheezed Vilnus.

"Seven, including me," Harrison answered, climbing through the hatch.

Vilnus counted six running toward the ship. The

ship was shuddering under his hand. Andrew was making the engines hot without the customary pre-checks. Three of the researchers made it to the hatch and stumbled to get in. Vilnus watched the remaining three, including John and Avery, running toward the ship. John exploded. A shower of red went outward as his legs crumbled. *Oh, damn.* Vilnus threw up. Avery and the other researcher ran up and slammed into the side of the ship, covered in blood, their faces a mess with tears, crying raw fear.

"In, in, in." Vilnus pushed them in. He jumped onboard and strapped himself down, fumbling with the straps as his hands refused to align. He prayed Andrew was a good pilot. *This will suck.* As his breath returned, he looked about, seeing that one of the researchers was missing from the passenger chairs.

"She's up with Andre," Janet answered to his confused look, understanding him. "I think she's one of their pilots." Vilnus nodded back.

"Five seconds to go, buckle down," a lady's voice came over the intercom. The hatch snapped shut automatically. The ship thrust started. And it started hard. One of the staff was still fumbling with their belt when the ship launched, and hit their body on the edge of the seat, causing them to wheeze. Vilnus thought of the trajectory out of the meteor shower, *We have to make it over to the other side of Horizon. Use the whole planet as a shield.*

He pulled up the exterior view of the ship on the display in front of his seat, arms heavy with the acceleration. The ground was ripping by underneath, and he swung the view to the rear of the ship. He could see the science center starting to go over the curvature of the planet when it disappeared in a massive puff, followed by a light that made the day brighter. Pieces of earth were flying up as rocks flew down to meet them.

He swung the view upward at the sky to see what the pilots saw and swore, almost bolting from his seat in gut panic. Seeing the rocks flying right at him was too much; he turned the view toward the front to see the motion of the ship relative to acceleration. The ship jerked left, and he saw a rock tear right past. They were still in the atmosphere but high and accelerating. Going up meant bringing their ship into a denser path of meteors, but staying in the atmosphere restricted their speed and kept them near the debris being churned up by meteorite impacts.

A hole punched through the top of the ship. The air screamed, making him temporarily deaf. They were all grabbing for the masks. *Air.* He couldn't breathe until he got the mask on his face. But it wouldn't go to his face. It danced around like a marionette, his hands unable to still it. Avery was wearing hers. Janet had hers half on, goggles askew. Finally, he managed to place it.

"If you don't have them on yet with the mask, vacuum goggles, everyone," the lady's voice came through the resonant speaker on the mask. He and everyone else fumbled, pulling the mask goggles up. Pushing his goggles on, he glanced over at Janet. Her hair was disheveled, uniform coated in dust and sweat. She looked straight at the screen, her eyes angry slits.

Vilnus stared over at the hole in the floor. The metal near the top hole, now auto-sealed by emergency hull gel, was losing its glow from the exterior atmosphere flowing through. He registered the radiant color of the aluminum interior hull, super-heated when exposed briefly to the external atmosphere. *Oh, we're definitely hypersonic now.*

◊

Janet opened her eyes. She huffed at the mask, trying to get enough air back into her system. Between the sprint to the ship and the panicked breathing, she was trying to get calm. This was horrible. Icy air curled around her leg, giving a little kiss of terror. A glance at the floor a few feet ahead showed a fist-sized gash in the deck plate. It belonged to a ceiling hole ten feet in front of that, like running through rain made of bullets.

They were still jockeying right, left, sideways, down, and up. It was sickening. The engine roar was fading slightly as they climbed into the atmosphere. From the engine's scream, they were running at a thrust not meant for this atmosphere. She shouldn't have been able to hear them, yet they were vibrating in her head like a pair of banshees. Things were heavy. Her arms, her legs, her brain. This was going rough, bad rough. She stared straight at the monitor.

The vacuum goggles had ear covers. She pressed hers and asked Vilnus, "Can we, can we get there? Can we get into the planet's shadow?"

"We're already hypersonic, fifteen minutes, I guess," he sounded funny. She bet they all sounded like idiots in this terror. It was nauseating and frightening at the same moment. Her stomach dropped, or the ship did; she couldn't tell.

The ship banked up hard, and she was pushed into her seat uncomfortably worse than they were before. A staccato of holes popped in from the floor to the ceiling. They were upside down, she now realized. And then they weren't. One of the researchers was screaming up front, or looked like it, with their face stretched wide in pain since he thankfully didn't have his comms on. Blood was streaming from his leg. Not good. The acceleration force was at their backs again. The holes in the ship were filling with gel.

◊

Vilnus was glad he had the goggles on this time when the holes were made. He heard the thump of the rocks breaking the panels, but his hearing was still impaired, and he didn't want to make it worse. His skin felt hot-cool in the decreasing cabin pressure. The emergency briefing started playing back in his head. *Breath slow, keep the goggles on. The ship will pressurize to pointthree atmospheres when safe.*

Time started slipping. This was not something you trained for as a scientist. *Do pilots train for this? Does anyone?* Vilnus thought.

◊

God, I'm glad we have an asteroid pilot up there, Janet thought. She thought it again, and again, and again. Something to reassure her that she wasn't going to eat a rock.

"We've made LEO on the opposite side of the planet, but we're not stopping here," the female voice came in her goggles, and the pressure in her guts backed off a little. "I don't expect any more impacts, but we'll keep our feet on the gas for another fifteen minutes to get us distance. The *Hooke* and the transport ship *238-Bonet* will be meeting us at L2."

Janet looked at Vilnus, who looked back with the same shock on her face she must have. "My luck," Janet said to no one, and closed her eyes.

Chapter 11. The Sun Is My Lover

Janet stepped off their lander onto the landing deck of the *Bonet*. She looked back at the chariot that had just carried them from the rain of death. Definitely a few panels missing. The paint marred. Looking closer, she noticed the engine mounts were actually bent. It wasn't going anywhere again without a rebuild. She looked at Vilnus; the color was returning to his face. He looked like he had run a hundred kilometers. They all did.

Captain Velasquez of the *Bonet* was there. "Please, over here, everyone. We have chairs if you want to sit, or please sit if you feel faint. Dr. Thomas, the ship's medic, will be looking over each of you." He walked over and spoke directly with Janet and Vilnus. "Drs. Avlen, Boren, and Harrison, I would like to get an out-brief from you at fourteen hundred ship time when the medic is done and you've eaten, please."

Vilnus nodded and stepped closer to Janet. He reached over and squeezed her hand. She looked at him and, with tears, hugged him and wept. "I think that's the single scariest thing I've ever . . ." she trailed off.

"Yeah, me too. I'm so sorry," Vilnus said.

"You didn't do anything," Janet replied.

"No, I'm sorry you had to be in that," Vilnus answered.

"Me too. Thank you." She stepped back and wiped her hand across her face. "Are you okay?"

"As much as I can be," he replied. "My ears are still ringing from the first hole in the ship. I didn't have the goggles on yet."

"I thought you sounded funny, like when you can't hear yourself talking."

The ship's doctor interjected, "Janet, if you could hold out your tablet."

She did, and the doctor passed his tablet past it. "Looks like you're not in immediate danger. Look at the eye reader here." He held up his scanner, nodding. The doctor asked the same of Vilnus. "I want both of you to drink as much extra water for the next twenty-four hours as you can manage without making yourself sick." He left them alone.

Janet spoke first, "I could have told him that. Anyways, I think I need to go be alone and change," she said.

Vilnus nodded in reply. He, too, found himself

in his quarters. And for an hour, his mind raced. He wished he had put his goggles on earlier so his ears didn't still ring. It was hard to second-guess still living though. Just the aftereffects of being in the event and trying to stop all the adrenaline, especially when it was totally out of his control when he had buckled in. He owed a thanks to those pilots. Then fatigue hit him.

**

Janet walked into the conference room of the research ship. Captain Amir of the research ship and Captain Velasquez of the ship *238-Bonet* were at the table. Dr. Harrison was just then sitting down.

"Please." Velasquez indicated a chair with his hand.

Janet sat. Her hands still jittered. It was unpleasant. Dr. Harrison stared at the ceiling, looking shell-shocked. They were quiet. Janet turned, almost startled, when the door opened for Vilnus. His face looked like he had run twenty hours but in his sleep. He sat down in the chair to her right.

"Captain Amir and I watched the video feed from the shuttle, from when your emergency beacon flared up to the point where the pilot cut thrust,"

Velasquez opened. "That looked . . . unpleasant, to say the least. To fill you in on the record, Andre offered Nalina the stick, having flown asteroids in research, but she yielded because he knew the shuttle. Nalina was the spotter, watching the asteroid paths that mapped onto the flight field for Andre to dodge. It's excellent teamwork and earned them both Silver Wings of Icarus. In case anyone here doesn't know, that's the highest pilot honor, and only a few thousand in the galaxy have the commendation. Nominally, there is a confirmation process, but simultaneous concurrence is enough for pre-authorization."

The captain continued, "Charly, who was hit by shrapnel on the flight up, is recovering. On regrettable notes, the death of John Armstrong is a tragedy. And unfortunately, the institute was destroyed in an explosion, presumably caused by a meteorite impact."

Captain Amir picked up, "We'll know more in seven hours when that side of the planet has spun to face us, as we're staying in the planet's shadow for now."

"I'm glad Charly is okay." Dr. Harrison leveled his head, his gaze a thousand meters away, "I'm going to miss John."

Velasquez replied, "Now, a lot of the research

at your center is about the dynamics of the asteroids in this system. Wouldn't your station be
actively watching?"

Amir answered, "Normally. Unfortunately, our
ship does most of the observation on this side of
the system, and its primary long-range array was
planet side for repair and an upgrade. And a few
days ago, the sunward radar observation post lost
one of its arrays. It wasn't critical to the current
research and happens from time to time on the
various observation points. We had a replacement
array for the sunward post ready for launch with
the sensor suit of our ship when it was repaired.
Whatever data we had leading up to this, well,
that's gone with the institute."

"Care to speculate on what did happen then?"
Velasquez asked.

Amir hypothesized, "If a large asteroid were to
pass in front of the planet's orbit, it could drag a
collection of small asteroids in its gravity pull. The
secondary rock fall could be devastating."

"And what would lead to having a large asteroid
on an off-trajectory course?" Velasquez pressed.

"It's an unusually turbulent system," answered
Amir, "but also, mind you, this is an illegal way
of mining in an inhabited system. But if a mining
ship were moving a large asteroid and lost control

of it or if the asteroid broke apart, that could lead to a run-away rock. There are a few mining ships out here. The asteroids are laced with small to substantial amounts of uranium, curium, and lesser amounts of ruthenium."

Vilnus caught a tick in Janet's left eyebrow at the mention of the metals.

"Horrible," Janet muttered.

"Yes, an early attempt in mining went very wrong and killed several hundred miners. So that kind of ended the whole methodology of moving rocks to the mining outpost. Especially now that technology makes it easier to just go to the asteroids and mine on the spot. But that doesn't mean it still couldn't happen," Amir finished.

"That would be a high level of negligence for certain," Velasquez said. "Any way we could reliably find out where the origin was?"

Amir answered, "I would surely love to, but without the long-range arrays running, it would take an extensive, probably weeks, search upstream of the rockfall. Then we would have to be vigilant about not hitting any fast-moving asteroids that are still in the tail end. And neither of our ships is set up for that kind of work."

"Indeed," Vasquez answered. "Any further commentary anyone would like to provide?"

"Just that I'm glad Vilnus is a vigilant observer so we could get out in time," Dr. Harrison said in a dead voice, and stood slowly to leave.

*

Janet lay in her cabin. Still, more hours had passed. She didn't want to see what destruction was down on the planet. It could wait, wait until the end of time. All she wanted was an answer to her first problem, not why, in general, the universe was delivering the fourth law of thermodynamics to her.

Sleep finally came to her.

> *Now I am become Death, the destroyer of worlds. She looked at Yasmin. The entirety of her eyes were black as night. "Janet, it is you. You are Death," spoke the disembodied Yasmin. Her form appeared as a haze with wings that stretched beyond the extent of view, another red eye blazing in her forehead, floating in space. A space filled with stars, stars that disappeared. Flicking out, one by one. She was falling through time.*

Janet awoke, hitting the floor. The nightmare fleeing her memory. It was ten thirty-four ship time. At least she had slept for her body's sake, even if her mind wasn't rested. "Vilnus, are you up?" she sent a text ping on her pad.

"Yes, on the bridge. I talked the captain into giving us bridge access as a courtesy. We're solar diving in an hour," was the reply.

"Other ship?"

"The research crew left last night, and they dove a couple of hours ago."

"I'll join you for the dive," Janet replied, and went to the shower.

*

The pilot, Johnny, announced, "Passing the Horizon 1 asteroid belt, interdiction line in four-teen minutes, dive in twelve minutes."

Janet had stepped onto the bridge a few minutes prior. She sat next to Vilnus at the observation stations.

"I ever tell you I like watching the dive?" he asked Janet.

"Oh?" she answered.

"It's like running into the sunset. Where space is the water and the sky both."

"You are waxing poetic. Please do not."

Vilnus frowned at her.

Janet continued, "I rather enjoy approaching a world I have never seen before, the variety of them all."

Pierce, the navigation officer, interrupted, "Captain, I have a radar return on a ship that is approaching our flight path. I think they were blocked by the Horizon 1 debris."

"Transponder, visual ID?" Captain Velasquez asked.

"No transponder," Pierce replied. "The visual system is acquiring them now. There is no collision possible, but they are tracking to approach us, really close."

Velasquez clicked Ship to Ship Broadcast on his console, "Ship merging on our trajectory, please identify and halt transit. We don't want any accidents mid-dive," he said into his communications station.

". . . Bringing up the image now."

Janet could see, just as well as the rest, that the registry marking was masked. The ship had asteroid-breaking panels up front and a set of tethering cable launchers for grabbing rock that could also latch onto another ship if close enough. The thing even had four atomic motors at its rear for handling and moving high mass.

Why mask your ship? Pirates, smugglers, not many

choices for a masked ship. Or someone wants to cover up a mistake, she thought.

"Pierce, could we outrun them?" Velasquez asked navigation.

"It doesn't look like it. The *Bonet* is lighter, but those atomic motors will more than make up the difference. We are properly trapped between those asteroids and any viable dive point. For our current route, we will dive from here first, but they will certainly catch us at the next system while we are looping to align with the dive to Kestrel," Pierce answered.

Janet saw Velasquez close his eyes in contemplation. He held his chin in his hand. She turned to the ship's computer interface and looked at their dive trajectory. A two-star dive through numbered systems, no outposts listed, and a thirty-degree arc around to align with the entry point for the dive to Kestrel. A normal passenger ship jump route. Kestrel was a populated system with an observatory, ships, and help, but with two unpopulated and unobserved systems in between.

Janet looked over at Vilnus, who also had a transit map open but scaled to dive times. "Thirty-four seconds, that's long, and six seconds," he said to himself. "Just grab us, pull us to into those panels, and throw the wreckage into the sun."

"What was that, Vilnus?" Janet inquired.

"Our future."

"No, throw us into the sun."

Vilnus snapped his fingers. "*Hastings* Incident. Look at the mapping." He put his fingers over the second part of the dive and spaced them over the first.

"But we are not behind them."

"Yet."

Janet stared at the map. She zoomed in on the middle star in the jump. "We could use the escape command, not the commit command, to get where we need to be. Not sure we will have the relative speed."

"Borrow it from the bad guys."

Janet looked right at Vilnus. "Captain, we have an idea. Are you familiar with the *Hastings* Incident?" Janet asked.

"That it was an accident of some kind?" Velasquez answered.

"Yes. Please put the dive chart on the main view scaled for dive time," Janet walked up and began gesturing as she described the idea. "One ship entered the middle dive between two stars at the same time as another ship passed it on a two-star dive. The second ship was gravitationally slowed and pulled back into the exit star when it emerged from the dive. It is why we have time maps. I propose we do the same. We exit our dive at the middle star and purposefully boomerang back but inside the interdiction line."

"And how do we get to Kestrel after that, or survive? We would be going the wrong direction compared to what you're describing. So wouldn't our momentum also be slowed?"

"Our own gravitational momentum drag will be extreme, but this is where we know something they do not. Thing is, we are diving between two numbered systems without transit stations. There is no timing authority. Each ship can only see the dive points when it reaches the interdiction point. We have the advantage of knowing the momentum changes ahead of time. Just need to have that ship right on our ass."

"They will also not be able to see our changes to course if they solar dive any time before we exit the middle star," Vilnus added.

Velasquez looked horrified. "You propose we break their momentum and set them up to be drawn into the exit star?"

Janet just nodded.

"I want another way," Velasquez countered.

"Captain, can I speak to you a moment? Privately?" Vilnus interjected.

Vasquez looked over at Vilnus to gauge if this could wait, but Vilnus's look said otherwise. The captain stood, and Vilnus followed him off the bridge.

"You must keep this conversation in confidence at Captain's Level Exigent Red."

Vasquez nodded, and Vilnus continued, "Captain, let me submit you are out of time and options. It is my estimation that the ship out there is, in fact, the ship that led to the deadly asteroid storm on Horizon. That it is here now to attempt to destroy this ship to cover up that event. I have evidence for Sky Patrol, that I cannot share, that implies that the malfunction in the monitoring systems was not an accident. This further attack on the *Bonet* will be to try to cover up a willful act of destruction and murder. I say this to you so you realize this situation is far more dangerous than it already appears, and I encourage you to take lethal action," Vilnus said.

"I, too, would rather not die out here. But I would like to consider if there is a way out that doesn't require me to make that choice," Velasquez answered.

"It's already been made for you. Consider where that ship chose to meet us. Without prior communication, without marking, and at a point where we have no maneuverability. And they waited until the research ship was gone, so each ship was alone. That ship could still catch the *Hooke* in the next system if they felt it also had to be eliminated as a witness. Also, recall that the research ship's long-range radar is missing, so there is no chance the researchers would detect either of our ships that far behind course. They want to destroy something we know or someone aboard. We are sheep to this wolf."

Velasquez narrowed his eyes at Vilnus. "I hate that you are on my ship." He walked back to the bridge.

"Any other options?" Velasquez asked of the bridge.

Silence was his answer. Velasquez sighed out loud. "Pierce, could Janet's plan work?"

"The main difficultly, given how close that other ship is, is we won't have the time to orbit the first star to realign the dive. Also, given how they are lining up, we would actually be lucky if they come at us fair and square instead of trying to drag us," Pierce answered.

"More risk than they need to take. They would prefer to use the tools that ship is built with," Vilnus answered.

"I hate this," Velasquez commented. "Janet, send all the details to navigation and the pilot stations. How is this boomerang performed?"

"That is the more interesting part of this predicament," Janet answered.

*

Six minutes later, Johnny was counting. "Ready to dive, in four—"

"Remember, you have to go for escape as fast as possible when the other ship's gravity wake is detected," Janet interjected.

"Three, two, one . . ." And then movement stopped as the inertial freeze hit them. Thirty-four seconds later, and they exited the dive at the middle star.

Pierce spoke up. "The other ship's mass signature is crossing through this star now."

Johnny ripped the commit lever backward past the central stop gate to the escape maneuver position. The freeze hit them again for just under a second as the ship's trajectory looped inside the gravity well of the star to the far side.

Janet knew it was just her imagination, but she thought she could feel the two ships pulling on each other. The inertial freeze let go, and the view opened up to the star, filling the entire screen. Thermal flux sensors came alive, blaring at the crew.

"HIT IT. Commit NOW!" Velasquez shouted.

Johnny slammed the lever forward again, and the

freeze took them for six more seconds before they emerged at the end of the dive.

Janet looked at the gravity map on her status board before it drifted away to static as they passed the interdiction line.

"There are no other mass objects in the transit path," Janet announced.

"Nothing on sensors either. It's clean out there," Pierce said.

Velasquez slumped. He then turned and looked at observation. "Janet, Vilnus, you'll excuse us while Pierce finishes plotting the route given our new velocity and we write up the official incident log. Ultimately, I'm glad that you were on the bridge for this mess, but please don't come to the bridge again. I've had enough. Whatever mess was going on in Horizon with that research institute, or asteroids, or pirates, or who knows what else, I'd like it to not shadow my ship again."

*

Janet sat with Vilnus, looking down at her cup of coffee, in the *Bonet*'s cafeteria. They were now halfway through the in-system turn to Kessler.

"Was Velasquez pissed or glad to be alive?" Vilnus asked, holding his tea to his lips.

"Honestly, he was probably scared to hell and

back. I know I was," Janet said, and sipped. Her hands had settled a few minutes ago, and she could finally hold the cup. "I mean, I just weaponized the *Hasting* Incident, something you could keep killing with," she said with a sweep of her arm.

"True, and I am sorry," Vilnus said. "How did you come up with that anyway?"

"My great uncle was on the *Hastings* during that unfortunate event."

"That's one way to remember history," Janet replied.

"Be in it? That's the hard way."

"Just like having to throw away some fundamental notions of what would be considered acceptable behavior," Janet signed.

"Anything you want to or can talk about?" Vilnus offered.

"Yes, no, and fuck me, I can't." Janet set down her cup and started crying in her hands.

Chapter 12. Are You Not Still Alone

"Yasmin, good job in there," Altan said.

"Oh, thank you. I . . . I feel they liked it," she replied.

"I think everyone did. This quarterly report to Research Directorate will be an exciting one to write. What you added last month was the ability for our clock to use non-linear interactions to move beyond the entropic limit for clocks."

"Glad I could help," but Yasmin couldn't muster a smile.

She walked along to one of several commissaries at the research institute. A security officer in yellow and blue brushed by her, but she didn't even notice. As her head continued to buzz with an annoying low-level hum. Her brain was insulting, most especially to her.

She sat, pushed on the menu for soup, and stared out at the sun of Challenger IV, and it felt sweltering, oppressive. It wasn't a hot world, and she was in a climate-controlled facility; the feeling was inside herself.

It had been six weeks ago when her world had ended. A new opportunity had been provided. It was not easy, this transition. After all, it was a total change of her identity—an unwanted change—and the pain was still with her.

The soup arrived, and she looked down, stirring her noodles. Little fragments of life in a soup of her mind. She thought it might be best to stop stacking up bricks between herself and hope. It would be easier to grow wings and fly away if the wall in her mind got too high.

Yasmin picked herself up and, while walking out, pocketed a little plastic knife from the dispenser. She paced down the hallway. Her mandated therapist time was approaching. She loved and hated it. "Theory of mind, but I am a trapped poet," Yasmin mumbled to herself as she absently played with the little plastic utensil.

"God help me." She walked to her therapist's office.

Dr. Sabin, her therapist, looked at Yasmin. "I see you have cut yourself again," she said.

"I may have." The blood was still drying on Yasmin's forearm.

"I would suggest another approach when your feelings are overwhelming."

"The anxiety drugs only cut it halfway, and tapping isn't distracting enough," Yasmin replied.

"And what story do you tell yourself when you feel this way, Yasmin?"

"I can't really say. You know I really wanted to come here when I arrived. But I feel that everything I say will be punished. This is just pressure, not help."

"Yasmin. I'm not interested in what happened. Nor should you be. I am very aware that gag orders can stifle recovery. But think about any other classified work you have done. If you were in a good mood, you would have no trouble not sharing."

Yasmin nodded.

"This is about what story you need to tell yourself about who you are, not what you did. I want to know how you describe yourself when you need to harm yourself."

"Me . . . I was betrayed. My trust in whom I was falling in love was totally misplaced. And that I helped in doing something unforgivable." She hit herself in the chest with her fingers pointed to a steepled point. "It hurts, like God . . ." tap ". . . wants . . ." tap ". . . me . . ." tap ". . . dead."

She tapped again with her peaked fingers.

"Some of these feelings will fade in time. But you have to work to accept that maybe you are not at fault."

"Oh, no. I am very much at fault from where I sit."

"Sky Patrol clearly didn't think so. You work here."

"I may not have done anything wrong, although I have. But it doesn't mean someone else will do wrong. I've invented a gun, it's pointed at innocent people, and the trigger is not mine. In fact, I don't know whose it is since I'm not allowed to know what I cannot talk about."

"There are many things that can happen that we don't have insight into. Let me ask, do you think maybe your God doesn't see you at fault either."

Yasmin stared at her with coal in her eyes.

"We've been circling that topic for a few weeks now. How does it feel to know you can be forgiven?"

Yasmin knew she didn't have that answer. It was her primary split—was she damned or forgivable? She teared up. "Hell with you."

"Yasmin, we have been working on something that seems to have you trapped. It's obviously something that is splitting your psyche and giving you a post-traumatic stress response. There is something I want you to do to help separate your issues with

Janet from your self-reproach. We will tackle one problem at a time. I want you to write two letters to Janet. You won't send these, of course. In the first letter, I want you to write about how you hate her. Everything about her that is wrong, disgusting, and vile to you. Write how she should burn in hell and shall be unforgiven in your memory."

Dr. Sabin continued, "In the second letter, I want you to write how you forgive Janet. List every trespass upon you and end each sentence with 'and I forgive you.' Use Janet's name. Don't just refer to her as 'she.'"

"That's asking a lot for someone who makes me feel like I violated God's first work," Yasmin answered.

"It is work. Work on the mind is no less difficult than repairing trauma to the body."

"I know. And I keep asking Him for some kind of answer, every night, 'Why me?'"

"Maybe you should ask a different question."

"Like?"

"Well, ask if you can have a new way to understand your events. One that is equally reasonable but where you're not a failure. Ask to be guided so you do not have to guess. After all, who could predict the future? You can't read minds. You are not a failure if you're not perfect."

Yasmin nodded. She had been through the list of her thought distortions before. She had at least been able to identify one false belief. But the others still sent her down a shame-to-blame spiral.

Dr. Sabin continued, "You need a different question to get a different answer. A new story to get you the answers you need."

"Do you think I will have a new question writing the letters?" Yasmin asked.

"That's very possible. But try it. Writing is not too different from thinking, and it will help get your thoughts out from inside you."

"Maybe. It helps when I concentrate on my work. The focus of it. Although I admit to just wanting to throw myself out the airlock sometime. But I think the pain would last too long."

"That's certainly a deterrent," Dr. Sabin agreed.

"Is there anything special I need to do to write the letters?"

"No, but use paper and pen. It will slow down your thinking. You'll also have the slightly more satisfying option of burning them afterward if you choose."

*

Yasmin wandered to her quarters coming back from supplies, where she had picked up two pieces of paper and a last rights box. She put them on the desk and threw herself down on the floor. Her thoughts darkened, and she turned and stared at the ceiling. She started ruminating and picked absently at her nails. It took an hour before she recovered her state of mind.

"Clocks, minding my time. Could have put me on long-range cartography, Sky Patrol," she said as she pried herself.

She took a pain reliever and sat at her desk. She pulled over the two pieces of paper that she had picked up, setting them on the surface of the desk.

Yasmin glanced at the desk surface and really noticed it this time. Running her hand over the cool duck-egg gray surface. She forced herself to breathe slowly. Pen in hand, she began.

> *Dear Janet,*
>
> *Damn you. I really mean that. Go throw yourself out of an airlock. It was selfish of you to go to my conference. How dare you even think I should work with you? I don't care if you really are the smartest woman I ever met. You ruined my life. And for all I know, you ruined the whole damn universe. Eat a giant rotten banana.*

Yasmin folded that up. She wasn't sure that helped but decided to continue the next.

Dear Janet,
I want to forgive you.

Yasmin stopped there. She wondered if she really did but willed herself onward, just as Dr. Sabin had said.

Work here on Challenger isn't so bad. I know you had no idea what you were doing. After all, who would want to ruin somebody's life if they're not psychotic? My coworker Altan complimented me about already being caught up on non-linear resonance for clocks as if I already knew all about it. What a laugh. Which, you might appreciate this, I finished the rest of my rest of my non-linear navigation program. Here it is . . .

Yasmin folded up that paper, too, and looked at both of them, realizing the voice in her head had stopped momentarily. She picked the papers up and placed them in the last rites box. Upon her death, the box was designed to carry the affairs inside to only one designated person.

"May these never be delivered," she said under

her breath. She closed the box and set the delivery ID to Janet.

She closed it up to forget.

"Buried, like my past," she whispered to herself. "God . . . maybe I don't need to know why. If you can forgive me, then grant me the serenity—" The door chimed.

On the door screen, a man stood smiling outside. He had on the yellow shirt and blue pants of security. Yasmin unlocked the door, and it slid sideways into its pocket.

"May I help . . ." She stopped as she noticed he didn't have a security badge and then saw the blaster he had pulled from his pocket. "You're not actually security. What do you have with—"

He kicked her mid-thigh, and she stumbled back. Yasmin's eyes widened in shock as he drew the blaster up and fired.

Chapter 13.   For Those With Startled Eyes

Janet griped, "It has been a while since we were here and I really did need a break. But you had the whole planet of Larado to pick from, why must you have picked accommodations where it is eleven thousand degrees out?"

Vilnus and Janet were sitting on the café patio of their lodging. The patio overlooked the nearby cliffs of purple-and-red sandstone of the surrounding desert. The air was cool, being early in the visiting season. A lighter white was the sky.

Vilnus feigned emotional wounding, "The sun rises on blue flowers."

"Oh, such lovely flowers for sure, but that makes no sense for why."

"Because the view is stunning, and it's not the promised forty-three centigrade of hot season."

"I will admit that. And at least we get real breakfast and not sad lodge breakfast. I hate sad lodge breakfast. One place I stayed while I was traveling for work charged me ten ration credits for oatmeal.

Ten, Vilnus! I always carry oatmeal instant packs on travel now."

"That does sound insulting. Were you on Earth? Oatmeal isn't popular outside Sol."

"No, I discovered it before my Earth trip. It is quite good on New Albuquerque also. I think you would like to visit there. The location was named after one of the prominent plants of their ecology, a large plant that looks like a white oak tree. However, it is not technically a tree. The cell type matches those of trees, but its leaves are support structures for nearly microscopic green mushrooms that have a chlorophyll function for the woody trunk and branch part."

"You have a real thing for plants. How come you did not go with plant engineering as a career instead of electromagnetic design?"

"Honestly, I took a botany class in college, and it was rather boring. The teacher called me out for poor attendance. I like owning plants, and I had a flight of fancy of being a farmer or a plant engineer of sorts, but it did not seem like a good choice. So here I am, designing field emitters and seeing what laws of physics I can bend."

"So no plants. What got you started in physics?"

"A preliminary school teach in physics. He was this goofy old man who would sometimes twirl around the blackboard saying something dumb about him and his wife or spouting historical wisdom. He was also very charismatic about the problems you can solve. I was inspired. Turns out I prefer design and engineering to experiments."

Vilnus paused for a drink. "So tell me about this trip to Earth shore if that wasn't where you discovered oatmeal."

"It was absolutely lovely. You should go see it. I spent a couple of days watching whales—" Janet saw the confusion "—giant water creatures that eat small zooplankton. They migrate, and you can go onto a boat and watch."

Vilnus nodded.

"Highly recommended. Also, it is a different experience from the pictures on wine bottles to actually see the green rows of grapevine in fields upon fields since they grow them practically everywhere in the nearby hills. As for the vineyards, I drank too much. How do you know about oatmeal but not whales?"

"I like oatmeal. On a trip to see a transportation museum with my family, they had oatmeal for sale in the gift shop as a novelty. So I eat it and now have it shipped in, the wonders of modern commerce."

"Thinking of modern commerce, were asteroid-mining pirates expected to be in the Horizon system?" Janet asked.

"I did not get any kind of travel pre-notice. But that is the point of smuggling: to keep it secret."

"I hope Sky Patrol finds some evidence to get those šūdas," Janet swore. "You think after three months, they would have found something."

"Possible they did and we just aren't privy to it."

"True. You know I like these visits, Vilnus, at least when we are not being crushed from above. Thank you for suggesting it."

"Me too. I'm glad you're still here."

"And you too. Those were some ragged couple of months."

"Don't tell me about it sometime," Vilnus said with a smirk.

Janet gave him a dismissive gesture.

"So, how is Texel Corporation treating you?" Vilnus continued.

"I actually like working for them. I am working on the production efficiency of their transport-class gravity drive."

"Different than your last job?"

"Different technology, given Sky Patrol's prohibitions. But same goals: make life among the stars better for everyone."

A butterfly landed on the nearby yellow flowers

and rested, its wings flapping slowly. Vilnus had toast and scrambled egg substitute. Janet ordered a salmon bagel to go with tomato slices.

"I actually think I like it here," Janet offered. "They made an effort to emulate an Earth feel."

"The blurb on the hotel construction in the lobby said they locally farm what they can without risking an invasive species problem. They mentioned that chickens, with their prolific births and ability to hide in the vegetation, would probably take over the whole planet if they escaped, and they would have to be hunted endlessly."

The butterfly left, and the waiter was clearing the table when a humanoid-style robot in a light green surface coating, wearing the red and gold of a physical messenger service, walked over.

"Excuse me, are you Dr. Avlen?" the robot inquired. "I have delivery."

"Yes. Janet Avlen. I accept delivery."

"Confirmed." The robot handed over the package and left.

"What is it?" Vilnus leaned over as she set it on the table.

"I do not know. I was not expecting a physical delivery," Janet said as she lifted open the top of the messenger case. Her eyes widened in disbelief, shifting back in her chair. "This . . . this is a last rights box. Someone designated me their recipient on death."

"Shall I?" Vilnus said.

"No. It can only be opened by me."

"I'm right here for you."

"I appreciate that. No one has ever designated me their beneficiary on passing before."

"The surprise of it is shocking every time. I've personally done two eulogies, and it has helped me let go. This will pass."

Vilnus shifted his chair next to Janet.

She peeled back the cover of the box, and inside were two coins and two letters.

"Two coins?" Vilnus asked, looking in.

"These are from Yasmin. The coins, she was religious." Janet set the box back down. "She is . . . she died."

"Is there anything in the delivery that suggests how?"

Janet peered back in the delivery box and shook her head.

"I do not think I want to know. She reacted so tumultuously at the end. Rather than using the event as a way to build stronger bonds, she felt as if her beliefs were fundamentally attacked. And after not hearing anything from her in these months, I have had no ideas of us being together again."

She looked back askance at the last rights box. "I am almost sure this delivery is meant as fitting payback regardless of the symbolism."

"It could have just been her place to store whatever is written. I have never seen anyone have enough paper at one time that they needed a filing place."

Janet picked up the first letter. Her eyes widened. She set down the first letter, looked into the sky, and took a breath. Opening the second, Janet glanced over it, slumped, and set the letter back in the box.

"Not good?" Vilnus said.

"Actually, I think you were right. These letters were probably never meant to be sent. She stored them here for safekeeping."

Janet picked up the first letter again, tore off a segment, and stuffed it into her tunic. The rest of the letter and coins she put back in the box. As she pressed the cover back down, the seal reset on the last right box.

"Here, please try to force this open," she said, handing it to him.

Vilnus took the box and tried to peel the cover, when suddenly it felt hot. He frowned and set it back on the table, and it collapsed on itself in ashes. "You didn't want the rest?"

"I do not need that kind of guilt. It was indeed

probably meant to be destroyed anyway. Still, this little piece helps answer a question that has been bothering me. With all the shit I have been through this year, this may actually be my answer."

They sat in silence for a few minutes before Vilnus offered, "Want to walk it off?"

"Let me just sit here a while. I am sorry, that kind of put me in a poor mood."

"I understand."

⧫

174

Chapter 14. A Banner Day

Dillon looked over at Oswald across the conference room. "To be expected, Oswald, to be expected."

"That's horseshit," Oswald answered.

It was the third time Oswald had met Dillon, the second time they were discussing the fate of Drs. Avlen and Invenes, and the first time Oswald had seen this conference room. It was medium-sized, with an elegant synthetic wood table stretching the length of the room. Clear white lights lit up Dillon from above, leaving the rest of the surroundings shadowed.

"Janet is very much under a security blanket. Sky Patrol has had at least one specialist shadowing her ever since she got back from Horizon, and maybe even before. I can't touch her."

"Remind me, why didn't you get multiple killers? You could have gotten both," Oswald said, flustered.

"We went over this in preparation during your first visit. You thought that the meteorite solution would solve your problem, and you apparently wanted the research center destroyed too. It would have been a nice practice run if no one had escaped. Which is why I helped you destroy half a planet. I like to be careful, so, as you put it, I have only one killer."

"Only one? How do you only have one for being in the arms business!"

"The rest of my security are for my goods. They aren't for hire in the capacity you desire. Nor would they be. I like to keep compartments for things. Makes my business plans more secure."

Dillon stood impassive, looking back at Oswald.

"And you couldn't hire more?" Oswald pressed.

"No, that really would spread out risk, especially since it would expose me the same way twice for the same goal. Establishing the trust of someone professional is not done lightly. I don't actually know who the agent is, and they don't know me. And even then, for the agent I use, there are three severable links between us that either of us could burn for both our security's sake. And no competent professional is going to get themselves killed on assignment. I don't deal in garbage, Oswald. I came from a planet of garbage. I won't deal in that."

Oswald sat down at the conference table and

twisted in the chair. "You know they have a security blanket? I don't know that."

"You may want to consider that because Drs. Invenes and Avlen are no longer under your office's jurisdiction, even tangentially, your access to their updates was limited."

"Why would they protect her? Avlen isn't Sky Patrol anymore."

"That seems relatively obvious in retrospect, and I will admit, should have been anticipated since you asked about both doctors. Security probably had a flag for unusual behavior on one or both of them, and Dr. Invenes's death triggered the security protocol for Dr. Avlen. With Dr. Avlen barely escaping the destruction on Horizon, I would not be surprised if Security had more layers."

"How the hell am I supposed to get rid of her now?" Oswald protested. "You're unwilling to use your killer, or you suggest they won't do the job anyway. The asteroid strike took weeks to set up and was phenomenally dangerous, even given the goal. And now, the diligence of such a well-known issue to ward against has intensified."

Oswald paused. Dillon nodded in reply to the silence.

"Well, what now? What am I supposed to do? Go

stab her myself?" Oswald said, running his hand over his head.

Dillon steepled his fingers to his mouth and put them back down. "Why not? Let us invite Dr. Avlen on a journey."

"That's precisely the opposite of what I want to do. I don't want to *see* her. I want to get her and all her mischief off the plains of humanity."

"Yes, I helped you bury half a planet under a trillion metric tons of rock. I think I get it," Dillon said. "If you were willing to go that far, why not go farther? Was that too high a price already for you?"

"A small price. I'd kill a hundred more people to save billions."

"Would you?"

"Yes, it's not even rhetorical," Oswald responded.

"Would you kill a million?" Dillon pressed.

"I would prefer not. At some point, this is hypothetical."

"Is it? You seem to imagine there are consequences that even Sky Patrol doesn't understand, and have taken it upon yourself to solve this problem." Dillon cupped his hands together. "To get Dr. Avlen on a ship of mine, I can place a special installation request on one of my transports."

"I don't see how—"

"I do have someone collecting information on her

still. She has gone to work for Texel Corporation. Works on their latest in gravity-drive upgrades that they have recently advertised. I am going to set up a request that demands her unique perspective. A Sky Patrol observer will be required to sign off on the request and participate. How about it be you?" Dillon said.

"What the beautiful kind of request is that? I want her dead, not gainfully employed."

"Still, you want her gone, and I want her to improve the transit possibilities of my shipping company."

"I think that's horseshit."

"No, not entirely. Do you know why I built this company?" Dillon offered.

"You like the money?"

"I do. That's not why. I built this company because those backward, shit-eating trolls where I came from deserve to die. In the same way you think Janet is a problem, I think they're a problem. They have corrupted half a planet with bribes, theft, and envy. I want to do everything in my power to isolate the Galtonian government and end Titus and the people on it," Dillon spat.

"That seems overly aggressive for a failed government and shady morals."

"Enough so that some agents burned my parents' shipping company to the ground."

"So they burned a building?" Oswald asked dismissively.

Dillon leaned forward on the table, eyes narrowed. For the first time, Oswald actually felt more than the usual neutrality Dillon presented. He felt ice.

"With them in it. It's not a metaphor, Oswald. By graces, I had gone out back to feel the night air; I don't remember the reason anymore. The part of the city where we domiciled wasn't a particularly well-lit or well-maintained territory. They came in the night. And it was done right under the noses of the local authorities, or with their help, who knows? But they came waving long blue banners with red bars, the sign of the local minister. Chanting outside my parents' house, someone threw a flash grenade inside, and then they proceeded to torch the place. My parents were blinded by the light of the grenade, and they couldn't find the way out. They used petrol and wax incendiaries, which stuck to the walls and furnishings of the house, overwhelming the usual fire resistance of modern buildings. I never knew if it was the minister, some competing shipping company, or the thugs on the street for not paying racket money, using the banners as cover."

Oswald commented, "Now I understand why the banners at the conference seemed to draw your attention."

Dillon nodded. "All my parents wanted was to build something from that miserable planet, and it killed them. I made this company from what was left of their assets after the barely functioning court system routed the funds. It was enough to buy a ship large enough to turn profits. That was the toehold. That was freedom. And with this little empire of mine, I intend to choke that planet to death. I watched my life burn, and I will have my vengeance."

Oswald stared at Dillon until he could hear his own heart, understanding dawning, and then responded, "And as you asked me, will you kill the good with the bad?"

"Oh yes, if there were a hundred good people on that planet, I would kill them too."

"And if there were a hundred thousand good people?"

"I would still kill them all. Good and bad alike. They both built that system. Or the evil work twice the good."

"And if there were—"

"All of them. I would burn it all even if it became a shining beacon of hope and prosperity. It came from sin, and from sin I will wholly annihilate the Galtonian culture."

Oswald sat back, horrified. "And what then? Should I bring Avlen to you?"

Dillon leaned in. "Would you kill a billion to save the galaxy?"

"I don't have to. If I link you and Avlen, then I just need Sky Patrol to—"

"Need Sky Patrol to do what, Oswald? The fact you are here and you have already killed tells me you don't have the options you want. And now you are not getting anywhere near Dr. Avlen. I helped you kill Dr. Invenes. Who knows who else you killed on that planet? You managed to get a ship and crew of mine killed; Dr. Avlen is a little more clever than you think. Whatever plots you think you are obliged to reveal about me, there are some serious ones you've already participated in directing. Maybe you should keep going." Dillon stared at Oswald.

"I didn't kill them, you—" Oswald protested.

"Says the man asking, pulling levers where he can in Sky Patrol, asking favors of me." Dillon held his gaze.

Oswald blushed in fury. "Seriously, fuck you. I don't owe you anything."

"You got one of my ships destroyed." Dillon smirked. "I think you owe me something, and when Avlen is on my ship and I have what I want, well, let's throw her out the airlock, shall we?"

"I don't like you. And I don't trust you." Oswald scowled.

"Oh, no, I didn't think you did. We are just spiders weaving a merry web. You might as well get the fly you came for."

Chapter 15. Everything You Ever Wanted

"Welcome aboard, Dr. Janet Avlen," Captain Sevelin greeted Janet at the airlock from Abeline Station Three to the *D'artagnan*. He wore the mustard-yellow fleet uniform of Eight Corporation with a peaked left lapel with "Captain" embroidered above a star.

"Thank you, Captain." They shook hands.

"Welcome to the largest mining transport in the Eight Shipping Company inventory. I'm excited to see what you can do to make our deliveries just that much faster. We will have introductions and an overbrief of the plan for the installation and test of the Texel Corporation's Keraline upgrade in the conference room. If you will follow me."

They set down the corridor from the docking airlock. The hall was a cool white lined with thin yellow guidelines knee-high. Janet noticed how small the telltale curvature of the descending floor and ceiling that wrapped around the perimeter of this sun ship was.

"This is an enormous ship. The four hundred–meter radius of the working deck gives you a different perspective. Certainly a step up from even the large passenger sun ships," Janet observed.

"Eight Corporation's largest. The volume is simply to hold cargo. Most shipments are efficiently handled by the standard-size cargo, but some transport, particularly those with dense materials and ultra-large volumes, are better handled on a larger ship. Since the larger ship has inertia issues in system, it's an excellent candidate for the recently advertised upgrade. We're glad to be one of Texel's early adopters."

"I think you will be pleased," Janet replied.

They entered the conference room. It was nicely appointed with faux wood panels and a black polymer desk for seating seven. At one end of the desk sat a man in Sky Patrol Planetary uniform, his face pale against the green of his jacket.

"Dr. Avlen, thank you for joining us. This is my chief engineer, Niachu, and her foreman Maurice. This is Oswald Osmond of Sky Patrol, Transportation Safety. He is here to oversee that all the protocols are followed for the installation of the Texel Corporation's drive upgrade. I am excited to see what this can do for our fleet."

"I am sure it will be satisfactory," Janet replied.

Niachu and Maurice nodded and smiled in greeting. Oswald didn't move. *Odd. Sevelin said Transportation Safety, but he is wearing the jacket of possibly Stellar Research, and he is missing his patch,* Janet wondered. She nodded anyway and sat down. "I know you read the brochure, but do you need me to explain anything?"

"I think it would be helpful to have some dialogue," Sevelin answered.

Janet began, "The gravity drive Keraline version one enhancement is a major upgrade to your existing gravity-drive system. There are a number of components for this system that must be assembled onto the drive. The upgrade does not ship as one piece. My manifest says the parts will arrive this afternoon. Maurice, I want to remind you that the interlock coupling, part three-eight-two, could potentially be explosive until we get it installed." Maurice nodded, and Janet continued, "Sevelin, our shakedown run has us doing a rapid transit to Elejon with an option for a second additional run to test the system."

"We will take the option. I'll have a new manifest request in from the central office just before we dive."

"I expect you will be pleased with the upgrade, and there will be no need for a tear-down."

"I don't expect there should be any problems. If, for some reason, the performance isn't worth the investment for the rest of the shipping fleet, we may well keep the Keraline upgrade on this ship at least," Sevelin said. "I'll leave you, Niachu and Maurice, to your work."

When the briefing was over, Janet left with Niachu, and Maurice got to the cargo bay to begin accepting the inbound parts.

Sevelin looked over at Oswald. "You can breathe now. She isn't wielding the flaming sword of Damocles around."

"I don't like having her here. She dangerous," Oswald declared.

"I think this will be a fine expedition. All we are doing is two test runs," Sevelin said, and left.

***

A few days later, Janet was lying underneath the housing to the Keraline upgrade, looking at the secondary interlock module and attaching one of the last wire bundles.

"Why can't ya just bring the whole thing assembled?" Niachu said.

"Texel Corporation does this to protect the overall assembly from being stolen and used separately from the intended ship. And it also prevents the manufacturers of several of the components from seeing the overall design," Janet explained. "You cannot take the assembly from the gravity drive as a separable item either. It is possible to take it apart, but not the same way it went together. This is basically a one-way assembly."

"Smart," Maurice said.

"We expect that major shipyards would eventually build the upgrade at assembly time. For now, it is a modification to improve the investment of existing ships." *I'm turning into a walking brochure*, Janet thought.

"Go ahead and notify Captain Sevelin that we have completed the installation in the expected time frame and we are ready for the demonstration run," Janet said to Niachu.

"Let's go to the bridge and tell them ourselves," Niachu said. "Maurice, would you mind staying here to monitor the drive directly?"

Janet and Niachu stepped off the swift ride from engineering and walked into the bridge section a few minutes later. It was an impressive bridge design. There were the usual navigation, engineer, operations, and communications crew stations, as well as positions for the logistics head, head shipping clerk, sensors, and backup stations for each crew. Mostly empty for the trial run.

The view screens swept around the full bridge. Even the doors disappeared into the surrounding view except for highlighted arrows on the floor to show where they were. Being a full twelve hundred–meter transport ship, the multiple stations weren't unexpected to Janet, but the three-sixty observation she assumed would be what Sky Patrol capital ships had. Captain Sevelin was seated mid-deck. He swiveled to meet the newcomers to the bridge.

"I take it you have finished the install?" he said.

"Yes, we are ready to begin the expedition run," Janet replied.

"Good. Mr. Perry is our pilot, and Kacela our navigator and stand-in communications officer. Mr. Perry, please clear us of the dock and begin transit to Elejon at full drive speed," the captain commanded.

Janet smiled. She fully expected this to be the response. The previous installation was similar. The captain of that ship had immediately tested the in-system full drive speed. The full-rated speed traded off some of the field shapes of a nice, smooth gravity field around the neutronium gravity well for the higher-pull elliptical gravity field. And on the way back had tried out the full max-rated speed, much to her and the crew's physical discomfort. This modified shaping tended to make people sick with vertigo as well as distorted the gravitational strength along the ship's periphery, as that crew had discovered.

A few hours later, the *D'artagnan* was approaching the solar dive point. Janet had a seat over by the sensor station.

"Well, we got to this point sixty-seven minutes from dock faster than normal. Janet, do you recommend we attempt to slow for a more typical dive-entry speed?" Sevelin asked.

"No, in fact, it would be best if you stayed at full speed. You will spend less time exposing the ship to thermal insult. And the dive computer is more than accurate to handle the speed," Janet replied.

Sevelin nodded and turned back to the helm. "Proceed with the dive at full speed." In a few minutes, the ship blasted through the dive point and was rapidly climbing out of the Elejon gravity well.

"Looks like we should reach the Elejon moons in about two hours," Kacela informed them as the sensors picked up celestial data. "This would be about one-third the time needed normally."

Janet was pleased to show off this upgrade. "Under a full cargo load, the transit time would be about three hours, half your usual transit time."

"Please continue to the Elejon moons and take up orbit when you arrive. Let's make sure everything stays nice and smooth," the captain said, and got up to leave the bridge. Janet went to work on filling in the details on the write-up.

*

Captain Sevelin, Niachu, and Wallace had reassembled on the bridge when they reached the moons. Oswald had joined them, apparently reluctantly, as he stood off to the side.

"Captain, what do you think of the upgrade so far?" Janet asked.

"It has performed without error, and the performance specifications are right on the predicted performance line. You have kept the Texel Corporation's reputation intact," the captain responded with a hint of praise. He walked in front of the captain's chair and looked at the view of the moons. "It has been a while since I have been here."

Janet looked at the five moons. They were alone without a planet, orbiting each other about their central gravity point. A faint yellow tinge hugged four of them; the fifth was emerald green. *Appreciably lovely*, she thought.

"This is one of the better screens I have seen. But would not the view be better from a window?"

The captain kept his focus on the screen. "This ship doesn't have any. Since we have a hundred thirty-eight outer decks, it is impractical for the bridge to have one. And on the outer hull they would simply be additional liability to give the cargo a nice view of space."

Sevelin stared at them for a solid minute before turning to face Janet. "And we shall test the assertion you made about cargo not slowing us down much on our next leg. I am sure you won't mind?"

"Not at all. Please proceed," Janet said.

"Navigation, please plot the routing for System C2C, and, helm, take us there at full drive speed when you have the route," the captain said.

Janet caught Oswald staring needles at Sevelin.

"Can I talk you somewhere private, Captain?" Oswald asked.

Sevelin nodded and walked off with Oswald to his office adjacent to the bridge.

"What the beautiful fuck?" Oswald growled as the door shut.

"They are beautiful moons. This was one of my early transport jobs, dropping off a supply manifest with some rock explorers. I wanted to see if they still looked like I remembered," the captain answered.

"No. C2C. It's a mining facility of quarent. And you know damn well that quarent is an embargoed material for any job hiring Dr. Avlen," Oswald fumed.

"Yes, but there is a shipment ready at C2C for

delivery to our disembarkment point at Abeline anyway. I am just testing the drive with cargo, Oswald. It is convenient. Why waste time or resources on a separate run or ship?" Sevelin said as he spread his hands palms up.

"I am using my authority to deny this transit," Oswald said.

"I am not sure you can. Nothing about Janet's operational role would have her interacting with the cargo. And per typical safety and handling routines, she won't have access. As the safety officer who signed the technical waiver, aren't you here to see that she doesn't have access? What are you possibly worried about?"

"You know I can't say," Oswald spat.

"Well then, you may file a grievance on technical grounds when we are back to Abeline," Sevelin said.

"We're not actually going back to Abeline, are we?"

Sevelin again opened his hands. "Why not? Anywhere else I should go?"

"To hell," Oswald said as he stormed out the door.

Oswald pushed through the doors of his quarters. Something was wrong; he knew it. Sevelin was right; he currently did not have operational authority, as he had indeed come as a representative of Transport. It was a guise, but it got him here. The problem was he had traded any actual authority for it. He didn't know what it mattered if Janet and quarent material were in the same place, just that it was one of the restricted materials that had been attached to Janet's prohibitions after the incident.

*

Four hours later, Janet looked out at the view of two mining ships. The further mining ship was picking away at an asteroid nearby. The closer, about one hundred meters away, was attached to their ship with three tethers located about its periphery. Its forward plates that guarded most of its front section from stray rocks glistened in the sunlight. From a red-lit interior hold, the ship launched small containers down another pair of internal tethers toward one of the cargo bays of their ship.

This could have been our rear view leaving Horizon, Janet shuddered. "I wondered how space mining transfers were done," she commented.

"Unless you need dock-to-dock sealing, using the tethers on the mining ships is most efficient," the captain answered.

"About thirty more canisters. Estimate we will be finished in two minutes," Mr. Perry said.

Janet had not been able to see the mineral type

but noticed that whatever the material being loaded was, it was incredibly dense, as they had doubled their ship's hull mass. *This will be a really good test case*, Janet thought. The mining ship released its tethers and pulled them back in.

"Loading complete," Mr. Perry said. "Shall I proceed to Abeline, Captain?"

"Proceed, full drive speed again," Captain Sevelin said. They rotated toward the sun, and the gravity drive engaged.

*

Two and a half hours later, one hour out from Abeline, Janet was on the bridge watching them pass one of the inner planets. Oswald had joined the crew on the bridge a few minutes earlier.

Communications blipped, and Kacela announced, "Captain, I am getting a mercy flag assistance request. There is a general call for ships that can handle three thousand four hundred passengers and reach the two-light-hour mark of System 147.228 in the next thirty-eight hours. The *Illiant* is reporting total system failure and just that much life support, including the escape pods."

"Navigation, what would be our arrival time?" Captain Sevelin asked.

The Illiant? Janet scrolled through her arm pad.

A log entry for a three-week journey to install a giant observatory. She could feel her stress building.

Kacela pulled the navigation screen display out to the whole front view. "Plotting now . . ."

The stars from their location to the *Illiant*'s reported location laced the map with alternatives in a duller color. The black path of their anticipated route shown in black on the pale yellow background burned into her eyes. She watched as the projected time came on the screen.

"Even if we reduced our current mass, we would get there in just over ninety-six hours. We have the capacity and the benefit of in-system speed with our upgrade, but we're three system dives away from the right dive point, and none of them are lined up for double jumps. I'm sorry, they would be dead by several days when we got there," the navigation officer said.

"Kacela, has the request listed any ships in transit?" the captain asked.

"No, according to the acknowledgment log, the only ship within the time limit and with carrying capacity was an already full passenger ship that would have run out of supplies halfway there," Kacela replied.

Janet had pulled up the stellar charts. She looked at the stars on her pad and started to tear up in frustration. They were indeed four dives away from a straight run, and none of the other routes were better.

"Options?" the captain said.

"Declare us station bound, as we will not be able to reach the destination in time, and we have an envoy that needs to depart," Oswald replied.

Janet looked at him with disgust and squinted at the numbers again. "The navigation computer is not accounting for the upgrade over the total route, just the current system we are in. The company wanted to install the appropriate update after the upgrade was accepted. Here, let me push the update to the navigation computer now."

She tapped on her arm pad and put the calculation update as available in the ship's utility queue.

"You will have to accept a primary navigation projection calculation change."

"Can we do that safely in transit?" Kacela said.

"All in-system calculations will be fully accurate. That was done at dock. The projection out of system will update separately. The calculation scheme will take several in-system runs to properly calibrate for different ship and star masses with time to traverse. There will be an accumulating error but one that will likely net to zero error given a long enough estimate route. Which we have here."

"Understood, Kacela, accept at your discretion," the captain said.

The navigator nodded, and the update began. The plotted route and time on the navigation display erased everything out of system.

"Dillon. What do you think you are doing?" Oswald interrupted.

Janet glanced at Oswald, who stood with his fists balled at his side, and back at Captain Sevelin, evidently someone who was actually named Dillon, who turned to look at Oswald.

"I am finding ways to save lives, Oswald."

"You cannot possibly go. You have no provisions. I implore you to stand down."

"We have air, water, and livable space."

The navigation display started drawing the route back in.

"Fifty-seven hours, seventeen hours over the requested time," the navigator read off the display. "If we use our cargo as a gravitational reaction mass, we can save two hours with a slingshot maneuver around Abeline."

"Close enough for hope. I would hate for this to end up a Sky Patrol dead-ship recovery," Dillon said.

Oswald looked at Janet, "Do you think that it is a good idea to go on an errand with a man who pretends he is someone else?"

Janet looked him up and down. He had acted with distrust to her the whole time and still wasn't wearing whatever badge of office he was representing.

Dillon replied, "Do you know how I keep people like you from ruining my company? It's because I personally check out new deals. If Dr. Avlen here knew I was the head of Eight Corporation, would she have been as straightforward with the test runs, or would I have gotten two representatives from Texel and an earful about profit increases, savings to route times, abilities to use fewer sun ships to get more done. It ma—"

"Oswald," Janet broke in, leaving the two parties in silence, "my dearest friend is on the *Illiant*."

Oswald looked at Janet with surprise, then back at Dillon.

Dillon answered first, "Behind this façade, I carry some wounds. I know what it is like to be left for dead. I go. My ship goes. Signal Abeline that we will attempt rescue and we are now under a mercy flag." Dillon typed into the console at the captain's chair.

The thud from Oswald hitting the door frame as he left punctuated the order.

"He's been at every one of Eight's ship upgrades

recently—I think trying to find more ways to fine my company," Dillon responded.

"Nice guy," Janet said.

"He really isn't."

◇

Chapter 16. At All Costs

"The atmosphere in central cargo is confirmed vented and hatch-ready. Auto-ejectors on standby."

Janet looked at the approach graph on the central screen. It showed them nearing Abeline. In a few minutes, most of the cargo pods of quarent would be jettisoned away from the ship and into orbit near Abeline for recovery. Slinging your expensive cargo out the back as a gravity-assist maneuver was a bit unusual; however, Dillon had talked Abeline Transport into it based on Eight Corporation having several smaller cargo ships ready in orbit that could go catch the cargo.

The central display showed an overlay of the system with the sun in the middle, their flight path around Abeline, and their oblique swing toward the dive position for their first solar dive to a nameless numbered star system.

The markers for the cargo bay pots clicked from green to blue to red for ejected and empty on the far right display. If she wasn't hung up on a bigger problem, Janet would have been astonished at the rate they were ejecting the cargo.

"Cargo ejected," Kacela said. "Solar dive in just about an hour."

***

Janet stared at the screen, watching the updates as they ticked in minute by minute. The ejection and gravity boost had saved them time, but not the full promised two hours, because the navigation computer said it would be beneficial to save some material for one more expected gravity assist during a realignment to the next solar dive point.

The bridge was empty. The minimal crew, which had signed up for only a one-day demonstration, were in quarters. The ship was performing a long automated transit around the red giant from their solar dive exit point to the next dive entry point.

Getting up to walk the ship and let out her tension, *The Illiant has really gone on a long trip*, she thought. *Breathe*, she told herself. *We have the fastest path. I checked against Yasmin's plotting program for non-linear dive opportunities.*

Janet entered her cabin to try to sleep. It was a fitful night. She woke in the same clothes as the day before. She washed and put on the second uniform she carried as a spare. Clean but not refreshed.

On her room display, she pulled up the larger star map rather than the navigator's plotting map. She moved ahead of their position forward to the next dive point and all the adjacent stars. Then the next. She looked over at the time to the target clock that was running. It seemed wrong.

Heading onto the bridge, she said, "The time-t-destination estimate seems wrong. It's been seven hours since I looked at it, and we are only down five."

Kacela tapped on her console. "We are indeed down five, short two from prediction."

She tweaked her face and continued, "Two things: the prediction for time in this system was optimistic. It turns out this red giant is a real giant. The star is frame-dragging the local space-time in its neighborhood. Unfortunately, the direction of transit we took was opposite the star's spin, and that is costing us."

Janet looked over at Oswald. "Sky Patrol Cartography didn't put the frame-dragging in the 4th projection maps. Why?"

Oswald held up his hands in surrender. "I'm not in charge of mapping. Let me look." He pulled off his arm pad and scrolled through. "The ship map says that no remapping of this system has occurred since that type of data was introduced to the cartographic system."

"What is the second issue?" Dillon asked.

"The relative speed improvement from the Keraline upgrade seems to have diminished. It looks like the three atomic reactors dedicated to it are struggling with the long-term output. You have nine on this ship. Bring the other three online but do not channel their input to the gravity drive yet. I will be in engineering to make sure the drive is not causing some kind of power surging," Janet said, and left.

***

There in the logs, reactor five was struggling with supplying continuous power to the gravity drive with the extra Keraline upgrade. She didn't see anything particularly wrong with any power feedback or other reason the Kerline itself should be drawing more power. It also looked like the power distribution system had an overheating junction where the distributed power network was over-concentrating current flow.

So we can add power with extra reactors, but we may lose if that junction goes. A design with backups but no overhead to deliver, she thought.

Janet left engineering and started walking the

circumference of the ship, looking at the signs on the doors. *Food storage . . . extra wardrobe . . . swift ride to upper cargo decks . . . Let us go float, take some pressure off,* she thought. She stepped onto the swift ride's platform and took a ride up to the low-gravity decks.

She got off at an upper deck that had a walkway and kicked down the corridor. Quite a different experience than the last time she was in almost zero gravity. The doors to the airlocks for the different bays floated by. She noticed the little indicators by each showed the relative height compared to the bay, the mass, and the class of cargo. The bay sizing had a pattern of large, small, small, large to help distribute mass with efficient utilization of space.

There are extra conduits for repair. We cannot add new power conduits, only repair what exists. We can only repair two of three power conduits in any given section. We have enough power sources. Janet kept floating down the corridor and pulled up the ship manifest, *Lead, why? . . . Chlorine, again, why? . . . Small amount of ruthenium . . . gold . . . uranium . . . What a random assortment,* Janet thought.

She headed back down to engineering and sat in front of the gravity drive. Pulling up the star chart on the wall display again, Janet centered it on the *Illiant. You are really far from your arrival star. That alone will take seventeen hours. With our delays, assuming we keep the power net running smoothly, I need to find twenty-two hours.*

She scrolled back from the *Illiant* to the arrival star, a main stage yellow star. She expanded the view back a little to the connected stars, nothing stood out. *Short to jump but land far, do not let gravity stop you from going near to far.* Back from that, a five-hour transit from the blue dwarf. Again she expanded the map to encompass a wider view. There, one very short dive away, staring back at her like a blazing red eye, was a red dwarf Empty-22.

***

Oswald stared at the side of his hurt fist from yesterday's bridge incident. He'd been manipulated. The distress call was probably faked, but he couldn't prove it. And he didn't have the authority to bar Janet from the quarent or any of the other materials onboard, especially not when they were under a mercy flag. Pretty much anything but murder was approved for rescue missions.

Murder. Oswald looked around his cabin and stared at his bag. He didn't have any weapons. *Can I overpower Janet in a fight? Possibly, I'm heavier, but she has three inches on me. Risky if Janet is anywhere near anything she could swing.* And he was aware she would be very wary of him for the display of emotions he hadn't controlled. Good bet Dillon probably had the computer tracking where the two of them were at any given time, and Dillon probably did have a weapon.

How do I stop her if she takes us all down the path to hell? I can't kill her. Kill the ship. It has the standard triple redundancy of every standard system. Oswald ticked them off in his head: *Public access so anyone can attempt to fix a failed system, engineering-only access for routine maintenance and backup, and restricted access that cannot be accessed except at port to keep saboteurs away and stop critical mistakes. So I can't kill any system directly. Critical mistakes.*

Oswald lay down on his bunk and closed his eyes. *What did the* Galileo *have that this ship does? No queer bird or whatever she called it in the proposal. Still likely using at least the quarent material. No excess thermal venting for cascade shutdowns, just the standard for this engine type. We have a Keraline upgrade. Shit, oh shit.* His eyes were wide, looking at nothing. *The neutronium core is the gravitational source.* Oswald's mind didn't think anything for several minutes, and then he smiled. *Yeah, I know what to break.*

A few minutes later, Oswald was moving all

the heaviest cargo he could find to four of the lateral cargo pays that lined up with the gravity engine's plane of the ship. *Can't lock the doors to the inspector now*, he amused himself. He wanted any and everything that was extremely dense—the lead, uranium, and quarent. Especially the last, as it was extremely dense and would probably weigh as much as the rest. He had been moving some of it with the automated pallet system from the central hold. But still, it was taking too much time to move it all before the next part of his plan.

Five hours later, Oswald found himself thirty decks down from the working decks where his quarters were. Without a safety override, the ship wouldn't let him go any farther on the inner decks toward the neutronium core. This far down in the ship toward the central gravity core, he weighed twice as much and felt very uncomfortable. Even some public access areas of the ship still required special assistance to traverse for any extended period of time. But he was in a hurry and didn't need help—and he certainly didn't want to have his whereabouts brought to Dillon's attention. But this was close enough to do damage. One of the structural stabilizer pistons was here, designed to flex the ship slightly and reinforce other parts to prevent structural components from being gravi-

tationally overloaded by the cargo and the pull of
the neutronium. He reached in and pulled out the
power conduits he had access to, including engineer
access as part of his inspector authority. *One conduit
should run it, two is safety, but in a few hours, this
will be very unsafe.* Or at least he hoped.

Twelve structural stabilizers and an hour later, he
was now one hundred decks up from the primary
deck and now weighed a quarter of what he normally did. Things were slow to fall. There in front
of him was the public access line to the thermal belt
on this side of the ship, all eight hundred feeder
lines of it.

Two hours later, his hand ached and was dripping
wet from pulling thermal lines. Fluid from some
of the liquid lines had escaped the valves and was
being wicked off by the fiber mat lining the cavity.
He wiped his hand on the mat. *Eight hundred more
on the other side. Take one down, pass it around*, he
thought, amused.

And six hours after that, Oswald looked at the
giant pile of objects he had assembled in one of the
lateral cargo stores. Complete with some thermal
line he had taken and rerouted to a metal bundle
near the middle. He looked at the emergency
placard on the wall, making sure he had not read
wrong the first time. For a fire, the ship would use

water suppression if humans were present and slow atmosphere venting if not. *Well, no humans will be present, so that will work just fine. Because who the hell on a ship tears off the locator beacons of the bleach and ammonia canisters and stuffs them inside a canister next to the spare aluminum and iron particles for the fabrication printers, and then lays the thermal feed right on top?* Oswald put his hands on his hips, looking at his handiwork.

He heard one of the doors open behind him, and he whirled. The lady he'd met at the briefing, Niachu, was walking toward him. "Problem?" he asked.

"Maurice said some of the aluminum fabrication rods were missing for a fix Janet was building. And it seems your ass has them. What in the mess have you made!" She tapped on her arm pad.

"Stop," Oswald yelled.

She glanced up at him. "Fuck your Sky mess," she yelled back.

Oswald pushed her over, and Niachu sprawled on the floor. He noticed a set of short metal rods at the edge of his pile. He grabbed one and swung down on her. She raised her arm up, and it cracked under his blow. She turned over, getting her knees under her to sprint to safety. Oswald swung again, hitting Niachu across the neck. She thudded to the deck, limp, with blood crawling from her hair.

"I'm burning this ship to its core," Oswald declared to no one and dropped the rod.

Chapter 17. Upon the Face of Darkness

Janet walked back onto the bridge. It had been a long eight hours, and her hands hurt. She glanced between Dillon and Oswald. Oswald looked like trash. *What has he been up to?* she wondered.

"I looked over what I could do to stabilize the power supply to the Keraline drive. Maurice was able to add a shunt to each of the spare junctions, and given human endurance, we can add another ten percent on our acceleration, but that only works the closer we are to the stars, and each one of these is not lined up to the other, so it is a small benefit. At least we have as much power as the baseline Keraline can use."

"Baseline?" Dillon caught on.

"There are modifications that—"

"You can't make that adaption," Oswald declared, "not now, not ever."

"I already did," Janet said. Oswald's eyes narrowed.

"So we can get there faster?" Dillon said.

"No, we can get there immediately if we detour to Empty-22. It is a two-light-year jump off the blue dwarf we just dove out of."

"Is this something Texel has been working on?" Dillon asked.

"No, entirely personal. And that's what I need to warn you about. If we press on as we have been, we are still twenty-five hours behind the *Illiant*'s declared dead point. And if we use my adaption, then there is a real significant risk that Sky Patrol will ruin your lives."

"Even with a mercy flag?" Dillon said.

"I really don't know. And I'm not at liberty to expand on details," Janet said.

"You really shouldn't use it. You will get us all killed," Oswald said.

"I don't think Sky Patrol is in the killing mood, Oswald," replied Dillon. "I said it when we started. If you need us to get to the *Illiant* for this rescue, I go, the ship goes."

Janet nodded. "Under solar dive operations, it is labeled as Commit Option Two."

Oswald had his fists balled up but said nothing more.

"Kacela, please plot us a course for Empty-22. Perry, get us there," Dillon said.

*

An hour later they had reoriented for the updated solar dive destination.

"Interdiction line in one minute," Mr. Perry announced.

The inertial freeze took place. Janet glanced down and then up again and looked around the displays.

"Something wrong, Janet?" inquired Dillon.

"That felt odd. A little too long of a jump," Janet commented.

Kacela spoke up from the navigator's station, "Captain Dillon, we will be passing Titus One in sixteen minutes." Dillon frowned and looked over at Janet.

Janet glanced over at Oswald, seeking to understand Dillon's scowl and the announcement from the navigator. "Is the Titus system not inhabited? We were going to be in Empty-22—"

"No, no, no, no, no, no," Oswald was saying. He took Janet's wrists and pushed them behind her, then started shoving her backward with her arms clamped behind her. He whispered in her ear, "Don't touch it, don't intervene. I've got the ship rigged. It will collapse when he runs the drive. This device never hurts anyone ever again, Janet. Just shut up!"

"You cannot use option two for the solar dive from here! You will kill all of Titus," Janet shouted right past Oswald.

Dillon glanced back. "I know. That's the idea. I hate them. I am going to kill them. That asteroid impact you got to experience, that was my first idea. But they have systems to watch for that kind of thing that I wasn't able to circumvent. This is better. I am going to just annihilate them. Their worlds, their civilization, their damn sun. All of it."

"You know?" Janet gasped.

"Janet, plus banned material, plus a missing star on the maps, and the bonus of pissed-off Oswald. "Let's get to ending the Galtonians, shall we."

"That is . . . wait! Oswald rigged your ship. We all die if you do this," Janet said.

"I also know," Dillon responded. "The drive will run first, and then my ship will reappear before collapsing in on the core. I brought the *D'artagnan*, my largest ship, on purpose in case the ship was compromised. I thought about structural failure due to an external ship injury; I didn't really expect sabotage. Considering Oswald's discussions with me, I suppose I am not surprised. Option two, as you called it, happens before the ship loses integrity. It does not bother me. I would be chased to the ends of the galaxy anyway. It's cleaner this way. I hang myself with them."

Oswald shoved Janet down in the chair at one of the auxiliary stations. He shouted behind him at Dillon, "You're going to die, and you still want this?"

"Same as you, Oswald. You keep telling me you would die to get rid of this invention, you would murder to get rid of it—and have, in fact. Niachu is dead, according to the health monitors, I presume from trying to interrupt your sabotage. Now we can both have our wish."

"I suppose fucking so," said Oswald.

"You are both monsters. You pieces of shit." Janet kicked at Oswald. "I did this to help a stranded, dying crew. My best friend is on that ship. Let me help them! I do not know your problem, Dillon, but Oswald, if you do not want this device to keep existing, well, tough news. Even without me, the risks and concept are out there."

Oswald frowned at her. "You say that. Your ship that you did the work on, I had it commandeered under Articles 23 hazardous codes and burned in a sun. The data center on Horizon 4 is buried under a billion pounds of rock. The entire whereabouts of *Galileo*, what you were testing, your reports, and all the data everywhere about your experiment were captured and burned. This ends here."

Janet was seething. Her mind raced as she looked for something to intervene with. She kicked again at Oswald, who stepped back but kept his arm pressed on her shoulder.

Perry stood up from his station and looked up at Dillon, who towered over him. "Sir, you said Janet had adjusted the course. I won't commit the ship; we can't use the alterations safely."

Dillon looked at Perry. "Safe? No. We can use them as I intended. In the beginning there was darkness, and then there was light." Dillon shouldered Perry aside and grabbed the dive commit handle. "Let there be darkness again." He shoved the dive commit handle forward so hard the end broke off.

Janet watched as her world shattered.

Chapter 18. You Quit, You Die

The world slowed, and she saw Oswald wince, Dillon break the handle, and Perry lift a blaster from his pocket and shoot Dillon twice. Oswald turned and took another pair of shots, crumpling to the ground.

Kacela dove at Perry. She hit him from the left, her hands around him as they fell on the decks. He hooked his leg around her and covered himself with a folded arm as she drove her elbow at his head. Kacela hit him again, and again. Perry rolled, dragging her with him, and shot her when his blaster arm was free from under him.

"What in tar—" Janet started.

Perry replied as he stood pushing the body off him, "I'm a specialist, Janet. I've been pre-scouting your assignments for the last few months, for your protection courtesy of Sky Patrol. I wish I could have gotten word to you sooner, but the *Illiant* distress call was fake. However, revealing I'm a specialist to everyone is a non-starter, blows the whole secret protector thing. And Dillon certainly had an alert if anyone other than the engineers went anywhere near you."

"I understand."

"Now, what the hell are we up to? Wait, be very careful what you say. I was told not to let you tell me too much detail. I just need to know what situation we are in," Perry answered as he stood.

"Are we actually at Titus?" Janet asked.

"Unfortunately, yes. Until I shot him, Dillon had total control of this ship. Also, with Kacela at the station, changing routes was not in my power."

"Can you navigate now?"

Perry nodded.

"And cancel the drive command?"

Perry walked over to the pilot console and placed a small puck on it. A little red circle orbited the puck.

"Afraid not. It's still locked," Perry answered.

"Can we navigate to any of the Empty star systems?" Janet asked.

Perry pulled up a star map display. "No. The energy build-up in the drive is, at best, a few minutes from the threshold marker."

"Any explosives grade eleven or higher on board?" Janet pressed.

"No, only up to grade seven on the manifest. So if

you wanted to blow the drive or the support struts, that's off the list."

Janet slumped, exasperated.

"Okay, look, take a moment. Any good plan goes faster than panicking. Don't tell me how. Tell me *what* you're trying to solve." Perry asked.

"Could strip you of your job."

"Janet, as a specialist, I have seen some gnarly stuff go down. I won't lose anything for it."

"If we do not figure out how to kill the dive program, scuttle the ship, or put this ship in an uninhabited system, we will destroy the entire solar system and presumably die immediately afterward as the ship implodes."

Perry stared at her with dismay. "I had hoped one or all of you was being hyperbolic."

Janet held up her hands. "No, I assumed we would be at Empty-22. And if anything happened and got noticed, then the record of how the rescue time was shortened would be wiped, like they were for my research ship. And as you heard, Dillon believed Oswald when he said he sabotaged the ship, so it cannot handle the stress we are about to put on it."

"Okay, pre-emptively destroying the ship sounds like the best option. Preferably without us on it. This ship is enormous and—" he looked at the pilot system display "—there are no other ships of equivalent size close enough. And I already know the nearest Sky Patrol capital ship isn't close enough. Let's see . . . I can't pick the sun as a transit destination to just burn the ship up. It's locked under the same lock-out as the dive program. No empty star systems anywhere near us. Funny, I can fly us anywhere but where we want to go." He paused. "We had another specialist shadow you since you got back from Horizon. Why were you there?"

"I was there to learn about the gravity resonance they were studying . . ." she trailed off, looking down at her shoes. Perry let her think. "Hypothetically, if we are well inside the dive limit, well past the interdiction line, the star might survive. But the lowest-risk probability is if we can get to a tight binary star system like Jason-Argo." She pointed at it on the star map on the navigation screen.

"How hypothetical versus how safe?"

"I need uninterrupted days to work out how safe. Instinct says twenty percent likely at least for a really compact star. But here, I cannot give you a number and the ship's self-protect will not let you get close enough. But Jason-Argo is practically guaranteed that there will be no side effects. Besides the ship collapsing," Janet said.

"I can't take you to Jason-Argo," Perry answered.

"Why not?"

"I don't actually know. Just that it's one of the few places on my do-not-travel list. At best, I try my clearance and hope we don't die. And there is no route, within the time we have, to Jason-Argo."

She pulled off her arm pad and started playing with Yasmin's non-linear dive navigation program.

"Here." Janet stuck the pad out at Perry. It had the routing to Jason-Argo plotted out.

"How did . . . ? Never mind. I still can't take you there."

"How many people live in this system, Perry?"

He poked the nav map.

"Six billion . . . Fine, Jason-Argo. But know this, if I take you there, your life will be very different than now if you have one at all. And not for the reasons you think."

"More different than being tricked into recreating the star-destroying condition that got my ass kicked out of Sky Patrol? Perry, let us go."

He turned and started working the controls. The ship began rotating to the new drive vector. Janet could feel the strain on her body as the ship's gravity shifted.

"Let's get to the escape pod. We're going to need the extra support of those chairs for the velocities you have on this route. And after that, to be off the ship as fast as possible," Perry said.

"Where are you sending the ship after Jason-Argo? Just in case it survives," asked Janet.

"Doesn't matter," Perry replied, leaving it at that.

They found themselves plastered against the escape pod chairs as the overpowered Keraline upgraded gravity drive pulled them toward the Titus sun at the human endurance limit. Janet's very essence hurt. They were under twelve gforces of constant acceleration after being compensated for by the ship's gravitational shaping. A hurtling star-destroying bomb rigged with a pile of chemical incendiaries was ready for them should they still be on this ship if they succeeded in diving safely. She could see the metric map being fed in from the ship's primary computer form on the wall status screen. They solar dove into Titus. Then they were skipping past two other systems, an unaligned six jumps in total. Forty-five seconds later, they were rising out of the center of the gravity well of Jason-Argo.

The ship stopped accelerating, and the gravity shifted to nearly nothing in the outer decks where the escape pod was.

Perry punched the communications button and said, "Perry, command special clearance Romeo

Romeo Juliet Vader. Target this ship for destruction," and punched the escape pod eject button.

They were shot out of the pod hatch, hurtling
forward in blackness. On the rear-facing screen,
the *D'artagnan* began glowing. Lasers from somewhere were hitting it. She could just barely see the
glow of a few molecules in space that were in the
way. The luminescence was intense, with nowhere
for the heat to dissipate. The ship melted in half
a minute down to a molten ball collapsing on its
neutronium core.

"Perry, I just realized. Why can we not see either
Jason or . . . What is that?" Janet pointed to the
display screen showing the pod's ship-locating scan.
Around the entire display was nothing but a wall,
an endless curvature of metallic paneling. It was
actually so far away and dark that the display was
reconstructing the wall from telemetry information.

"I don't know. I've never been briefed on what
is here. But we didn't die, so apparently we get to
find out."

The escape pod approached the edge of the massive wall and passed into it. They were grappled on
two sides and towed upward for what seemed like
kilometers. After an hour, they stepped out into a
gray airlock with amber-white illumination.

Two Sky Patrol guards stood there with blasters in hand. They were dressed in emerald-blue and black tunics, with a thin filigree of red running up the left arm and two yellow diagonal strips on the front right shoulder of security.

"Who are you?" one asked.

"Specialist Perry Allen. You have my code."

"I am Dr. Janet Avlen."

They handed their pads over to the men, who examined their credentials. The pads were put in a black satchel on the hip of one guard. Perry turned over his blaster, which went in the bag the other guard was wearing.

"And what do we do with you, Perry?"

"I won't be needed from here on. I'll take the gag order briefing and leave as permitted."

"And of Janet, Perry?"

"I suggest you brief her. Janet has an amazing ability to work with gravity drives well beyond anyone alive, but approve all her travel plans. She is not quite safe in the wild. But I am also sure she is adaptable to other scientific work."

"Okay, we will let the head researcher decide. Please follow me, Janet. Perry, Guard Thirty Four will take you to a quick briefing and then the Sky Patrol ship on duty for escort out."

The guard took Janet to an unusually shaped

swift ride. On the walk to it, she noticed the ship's style. It was new to her. The control panels were all lower to the ground. Lot s of gray and moss-green coloration was used. The deck plates were very smooth with little texture. The painted-on lettering made no sense, and all the screens were blacked out as she passed.

They took several more swift rides and passed through several more hallways until they reached the conference room. Janet sat in one of the empty chairs at a table with five sides. An older-looking man entered and sat at one of the other sides of the table. He was wearing the same tunic as the guard but no blaster or yellow strips on the right. His tunic had two stacked double gold bars over the left arm filigree.

Commodore of what? Janet thought.

"Dr. Janet Avlen. Your record, if true, is impressive. And if not true, probably more impressive. Brought here by a specialist who focuses on asset protection and extraction. That is despite him knowing that it was a gambit on your lives."

Janet started to speak, but the unknown commodore raised his hand to stop her.

"I read the statement Perry gave to the guard. His testimonial about you is solid. You have no gag order violations listed, and it is a very long order by any standard. No direct attempt to access restricted material on file either.

"I'm going to ask you if you are willing and able to keep silent about everything you ever see or learn at this facility. Violating that which will be stated in your acceptance notice will not be imprisonment in the normal sense, but you will be either captured and contained or assigned death without trial or notice."

"That is a rather sharp consequence. Maybe you can tell me where I am, to take this bargain?" Janet asked.

"A Sky Patrol facility."

"I've been excommunicated."

"Yes, but you can be invited back in."

"What will I do if I accept?"

"Research on the unknown."

"Will I always be at this facility, or will there be other assignments?"

"A lifelong four hundred–page gag order that even I can only see the summary of. Escaping from asteroid pirates. A meteorite storm. Reinventing yourself twice in your career. And then crashing a thousand-meter ship into a Sky Patrol do-not-travel zone, using an unheard of navigation methodology from an obscure and incomplete research paper by a Dr. Invenes, whom, according to your records, you never met."

Janet winced briefly in reaction.

The commodore continued, "You have met her then. So you do have redacted records. I actually think you will like Special Research."

Janet replied, "As of now, I think Perry will make sure I do not have a job with Texel Corporation anymore, or any other gravity drive work. So that will be my third career reinvention. Let me read the acceptance notice."

The unknown commodore handed her a tablet. Janet looked especially for what she would learn or have to conceal, but the notice letter was vague on what not to say, just nothing about what was at Jason-Argo. It took her thirty minutes to read it all.

"I do not have my pad anymore. How do you want me to credential this?"

The commodore produced an arm pad. "With this."

She looked it over. It was, again, another new pad. It only had a credential string on it. Janet raised it and her eyebrow in question.

"The rest will be filled in upon acceptance."

Janet put on the arm pad, gave it her prints, scanned both eyes, proceeded to tap it against the letter, and affirmed the notice with one more eye capture.

"Welcome to Sky Patrol Special Research. Specifically project Interpretation. I'm Commodore Theodosius Tzu. I'm rather glad you decided to join us. I could not have let you live otherwise."

"What!"

"I'm sure Perry mentioned that this site was marked for lethal response. There's the getting here part, which you did. Then there is the protecting part, which you just agreed to. Project Interpretation is covered by a protocol known as Whispering-Butterfly. Named after Lorenz-Bradbury's simplification facilitate, the understanding of the concept of small-perturbation behavior in chaos theory, Whispering-Butterfly seeks to prevent the effects of information leaking out by stamping on the leaks.

"I am glad to have not fallen afoul of that before."

"With your altered history, there are higher protocols in Sky Patrol that you are unaware of that have already affected you."

"I understood that to some degree before. Let us switch subjects from my golden pardon. Where are we?"

"It's a cylinder. It's not ours, either. The Ermei live on it. You'll meet one soon enough."

"The who?" Janet asked.

"Alien species."

"We know aliens?" Janet blurted.

"Only the Ermei. Only ones Sky Patrol knows of."

"That is fantastic. How long has Sky Patrol known?"

"About four years. Discovered during a recharging run."

"Why do you not let people know, why Whispering-Butterfly?"

"The political implications are totally unknown. Everything from better unification against the other to madness as trust breaks down. Not all reasons are governmental either. The researchers I'm going to introduce you to will give you more sympathy for the Ermei's predicament."

*

"I'm Dr. Barrett, and this is Watts. Let us walk and talk," the researcher introduced himself and his colleague, and motioned her to follow. Commodore Tzu excused himself and left with the guard.

"So, Janet, this whole structure is a habitat, a giant space station. As far as we can tell, it isn't designed to travel from place to place around solar systems. It does, however, seem to dive, but without momentum through a gravity well as is required of solar diving."

Janet, shocked, interrupted, "It does what?"

"It zero-momentum dives. We think it's a property of being in this binary system, but we have no data to support that. Neither do the Ermei. They don't understand all of their station's systems anymore. They have a long-running story of many zero-momentum dives, but somewhere past four thousand chart-counting time increments, their history dies off and the station's data is not accessible much farther back."

"They did it."

"Did what?"

"Nothing, the concept is fascinating," Janet recovered. "How many of them are there?"

"They're half the population they used to be. Two hundred million live here, but still half. They work on maintenance and preservation. We don't understand what is happening either. Just that their records that they do have show that regularly, every ten years, this station dives out of Jason-Argo to a system the Ermei call 'Bokep,' translated as 'linked place,' Ermei's link, if you want. The next transition is in six days. Then four years later the station will dive back to here. If you have a much deeper insight into this setup than our experts, then the Ermei would be grateful. And so would Sky Patrol for helping a new ally."

Janet answered, "A fascinating problem, to be sure. What do the Ermei look like?"

"Why don't you meet Rodger-Bogger, our chief liaison."

They arrived at another conference room with a five-sided table. Janet sat, and Watts showed the layout of the station. It was a Dyson cylinder, large enough to surround an ultra-compact dwarf star or extra-sized gas giant. Except in Jason-Argo, its gravity was pulled outward from the axis. The Sky Patrol envoy vessel Odoric was at the midline, a small dot by comparison to the massive station. The humans all lived on the ship, with spill over working areas at docking. The rest was all Ermei territory.

Rodger-Bogger arrived. He was about as green as promised, four feet tall, and cone shaped. He walked in on his two arms using his fists as feet, and set himself down near the table's edge. He was dressed in yellow robes and had a satchel about him.

"I am Roger-Bogger. You are?" he said, offering Janet his hand.

"Dr. Janet Avlen. I am new here. You shake hands?"

"No, some of my mannerisms I do for your customs. I hope you can help, that you may add to the satchel of wisdom. The reference is obvious, but it's a long, traditional greeting of my people. We don't have separate leg units like you, so we must carry with us tools to use and stones to fling in defense. We do not have fist fights, as you might guess." Roger-Bogger made what looked like a giant open smile like he was going to eat cotton candy.

"I hope to add to the satchel," Janet replied.

*

After a while, Dr. Barrett led Janet outward toward the docking area.

"This is fantastic. So why don't you tell people they exist?" Janet asked.

"A few reasons. The Ermei are essentially stuck. They can't leave here, but just as importantly, they can't flee, and we don't want the whole galaxy of humans trying to visit. There is nothing in the connecting star systems of interest, and for guarding the site, we do have waypoint stations on route. How you got here was definitely new. Eventually, we may let people know, but for now, it doesn't matter," Barrett stated.

"I am very interested in their problem. It is really telling that this cylinder station jumps from here and there on its own. And you have never matched the star pattern or gravity map at Bokep?" Janet asked.

Barrett shook his head. "No, it is nowhere near anything Sky Patrol has mapped. It is a shame you arrived so near departure. However, they will be back soon enough, and the dataset we collected this time is fairly large. You can also get specialized training to leave the satchel area, as the Ermei named our agreed common area, and interact with the rest of the station and population."

Janet nodded and felt like she was about to nod off. "Okay. I am exhausted. Maybe I should berth up then?"

Barrett escorted Janet to the Sky Patrol envoy ship. As they approached, the access door to the ship opened. In the door stood Vilnus.

Chapter 19. Don't Be a Stranger

"Vilnus . . . May the heavens actually guide me. I thought you were on the *Illiant*. What are you doing here?"

Barrett spoke up, "You know each other?"

Vilnus replied without moving his gaze from Janet. "You didn't tell her that I was here?"

"Tell her? That would have been the commodore's job," Barrett replied.

Vilnus answered, "We are on the *Illiant*. It's the cover name for here," he replied.

Janet's face fell open. "Son of a bitch. Do you know how close I came to getting a solar system destroyed? I thought you were going to die!"

"Slow down a little. You're not alone here. I'm listening." He opened his arms.

Janet fell into Vilnus's embrace and felt sick.

The warmth in her breath and shaking brought time to a slow hum. Vilnus noticed that Barrett had politely left them to be alone in the corridor.

"Destroy a solar system?" Vilnus asked, holding her slightly away so he could see her face.

"I rebuilt Sunspot."

Vilnus shook his head gently, not understanding.

"From my research just after grad school, remember? I mentioned it on that walk in the Walker gardens."

Vilnus nodded this time.

"It is too dangerous. It always was. The last contractor that hired me, their president faked a distress signal from the *Illiant*," Janet answered.

"Oh, dear Janet." Vilnus hugged her again. "I am glad you are here."

She sobbed oceans into his tunic then.

***

Vilnus met Janet the next day for lunch in the Odoric cafeteria. He watched as she entered wearing the emerald-blue and black tunic with the thin filigree of red running up the left arm. She now matched the rest of the Sky Patrol members wearing the uniform of Special Research members when on assignment.

"What has the research team kept you busy with this morning?" he asked.

"It was decided since the Ermei station transits in just five days that I should follow the gravity drive and mapping team around with an Ermei named Don-Thunder. I wish I knew where they picked their names from."

"They do seem to have some humor, if unintended. Pick up any new clues?"

"No, and I am wishing I had more time in person. This is all so fantastically new. Did you know they have no neutronium core?"

"I did not. My main focus here was their communications systems. Or maybe more specifically, how they don't seem to have a long-range system. But their passive sensors for any electromagnetic emissions are truly massive. Seems they listen more than broadcast."

"It is fascinating what they let us see. So much to learn. When did you get into Special Research?"

"Not long before Horizon. It was that new job in Sky Patrol I hinted at but couldn't go into."

"No more hinting, hiding, and covering?"

"Now that we are both in deadly butterfly—" Vilnus rolled his eyes briefly "—no."

"It will be a relief to have a friend again, who can know your struggles. I lost that when Yasmin departed."

"I understand. Comradery is not the same as true friends."

They ate and headed out for the day.

***

Vilnus met Janet again the next day for lunch. And again on the third day. This time she entered with her uniform and an additional moss-green sash tied to her waist with a blue satchel at her side.

"I see you have been honored by the Ermei," Vilnus commented.

"Yes. I was told I was the second researcher to receive such a gift," Janet beamed.

"It looks good with the uniform. You seem a little happier today."

"There is something peaceful on this ship. I do not know if it is because they have been stuck for so long that they have this lackadaisical way of behaving, or if it is their natural behavior."

"The xenopology section of the research is really light. Even with the training, only a few researchers are allowed on the neighboring ship sections."

"That changed today. I was escorted off to one power conduit away from the known areas. They wanted some maintenance, just one or two turns on a crank, that was totally out of reach for them. I guess whatever lever used to be used has been lost. And you know they will not accept any maintenance robot, no matter how simplistic."

Vilnus raised his eyebrow and nodded in appreciation. "I do wonder why they won't take at least one for uninhabitable zones or repair."

"More things to learn. It seems it will take some time for them to be open with us."

"I guess we will learn what we can while we are here. Shall we?" Vilnus said as he stood up.

Janet smiled and walked with him out to the ship.

***

Three days later, dive day. The Sky Patrol vessel Odoric had detached from the Ermei station and station keeping near Argo. Vilnus was on the bridge watching the Ermei cylinder glowing as it prepared to dive.

"Janet, you may want to see this," Vilnus typed into his pad.

"I am watching. This moment is one I am not going to miss," came the reply.

The cylinder zero-momentum dived as promised, and the glow in space faded.

The navigator commented, "No response from the gravity drive that is not of compensation for changes in the metric from the change local mass from the Ermei diving."

"Were you expecting one?" Vilnus asked.

"Just a note. We have no idea how zero-momentum dives work."

Vilnus left the bridge and headed to his cabin for the transit. Once he was inside, a message alert arrived. It was a proximity message from Janet. Pulling his pad off his arm and reading, he sat on the bed, and his head slumped, and set the pad beside him.

> *Dear Vilnus,*
> *You are my best friend. But the last year has been rough. You have ridden some of it with me, and I thank you. This ship offers me something, peace. I love you, and I hope you understand. That I just need some space.*

Acknowledgements

Thank you to my wife, who was very supportive in the finishing of this book. And thank you also to my friends Andy and Mark, who helped motivate key people in this book. No thanks to some that helped motivate other characters.

About the Author

James Leland grew up in sunny place USA. He has a doctorate in physics from a school in Massachusetts.

Despite the complaints of several English teachers, James wrote short stories and a mini-novel in high school. His writing was reformed by Strunk and White. Spontaneous poetry is also written.

This is his first published work in sci-fi. Hope you enjoyed!

Milton Keynes UK
Ingram Content Group UK Ltd.
UKHW041419071024
2034UKWH00001BA/1

9 798990 130906